The Dangers for Spies

Hearts in Hazard ~ Book 5

By

M. A. Lee

WRITERS INK BOOKS

The Danger for Spies
Copyright © 2017
Emily R. Dunn / Doing Business as M. A. Lee & Writers' Ink

First electronic publishing rights: March 2017

Published in the United States of America.

Cover Design by Deranged Doctor Design

Contact ~ www.writersinkbooks.com and winkbooks@aol.com

Note to the Reader

When I wrote *A Game of Spies*, I fell in love with the character of Toby Kennit. He met the love of his life, Melly Ratcliffe, in that novel, yet Toby demanded to appear in another story ~ especially after his friend Gordon, Lord Musgrove received his own story in *The Danger of Secrets*.

When I began writing this story, Eugenie DesChamps sprang onto the page fully formed. She demanded equal time with Toby—as well as her own love story and her own danger. *The Dangers for Spies* also contains some rather dark scenes, all associated with Didier Poulaine, a man whose need for revenge turns him a dark operative who enjoys his work too well.

This story is one of the shortest in the **Hearts in Hazard** series, more like a novella than a novel. I trust you enjoy this *Dangers for* Spies that Eugenie dictated onto the page.

The interconnected stories about French spies are these ~

A Game of Secrets, which introduces the smugglers and the courier used by the French spy ring.

A Game for Spies, which brings the hunt for the French courier to its end.

The Dangers for Spies, this story, with its wider circle of French spies in London,

aand *The Hazard for Spies,* the conclusion of the conflict.

Novels by M.A. Lee

The Hearts in Hazard series
A Game of Secrets
A Game of Spies
A Game of Hearts

The Dangers of Secrets
The Dangers for Spies
The Dangers to Hearts

The Key to Secrets
The Key for Spies
The Key with Hearts

The Hazard of Secrets
The Hazard for Spies
The Hazard with Hearts

Post-World War I mysteries
Digging into Death
Christmas with Death
Portrait with Death (coming soon)

Non-Fiction Works

Think like a Pro Writer series
Think like a Pro ~ 1
Think / Pro: A Planner for Writers ~ 2
Old Geeky Greeks: Write Stories with Ancient Techniques ~ 3
Discovering Your Novel ~ 4
Discovering Characters ~ 5
Discovering Your Plot ~ 6
Discovering Your Author Brand ~ 7
Discovering Sentence Craft ~ 8

*Just Start Writing ~ **Inspiration 4 Writers** :: book 1*

2 * 0 * 4 Lifestyle: A Planner for Living

Table of Contents

The Dangers for Spies   1

Note to the Reader   3
Novels by M.A. Lee   4
Non-Fiction Works   4
Table of Contents   5
Prologue ~ 1810 July ~ London ….. 7
Chapter 1 ~ Monday, 24 February 1812 ….. 14
Chapter 2 ~ Friday, 28 February 1812 ….. 27
Chapter 3 ~ Monday, 2 March 1812 ….. 32
Chapter 4 ~ Tuesday, 3 March 1812 ….. 39
Chapter 5 ~ Wednesday, 4 March 1812 ….. 48
Chapter 6 ~ Friday, 6 March 1812 ….. 57
Chapter 7 ~ Wednesday, 11 March 1812 ….. 63
Chapter 8 ~ Thursday, 12 March 1812 ….. 72
Chapter 9 ~ Friday, 13 March 1812 ….. 85
Chapter 10 ~ Sunday, 15 March 1812 ….. 95
Chapter 11 ~ Wednesday to Friday, 19 to 21 March 1812…109
Chapter 12 ~~ Friday to Saturday, 21 to 22 March 1812 … 117
Epilogue ~ Saturday, 22 March 1812 ….. 126
Thank You! ….. 129
French Spies Threaten British Lives ….. 131
1st Book ~ A Game of Secrets ….. 131
2nd Book ~~ A Game of Spies ….. 131
3rd Book ~~ The Dangers for Spies …..132
4th Book ~~ The Hazards for Spies ….. 132
Hearts in Hazard by M.A. Lee ….. 133
The **Into Death** Series, set after World War I ….. 134
Nonfiction by M.A. Lee ….. 135
Pen Names of M.A. Lee ….. 137

Prologue ~ 1810 July ~ London

The door opened. Eugenie remained as she was, staring through the rain-drenched window at the garden. If she were to die here, the only place in the world where she had expected safety after six years of hiding, then so be it. She had wearied of running.

A footstep, then the door closed. More footsteps, quickly muffled by the flat-weave carpet covering the wax-sheened floor.

Had she been in Paris, pretending to be Madame de la Croix, she would have greeted the incomer with a glittering smile and effusive chatter. Had she been in Brussels or Dusseldorf or Groningen, she would have surreptitiously drawn her little pistol then waited to see if the intruder were a thief or a murderer. Yet she was in London, at Sir Roger Nazenby's residence in exclusive Mayfair, and she took neither of those actions.

He stopped several steps away. Was he innately wary? Or had caution come after years as England's great spycatcher? Eugenie had given no name to the servant. She had almost expected to be refused entrance. Yet the bruiser serving as doorman had admitted her without question. Apparently, mysterious visitors often came to Sr. Roger's door. And the mantilla and voluminous cloak that shielded her identity had not twitched a single of his whiskers.

The silence grew heavy before he spoke. "Madam, you wished to speak with me?"

Either the servant hadn't conveyed her name or the great English spycatcher would not use it until he confirmed her identity himself.

"I do." Turning from the window, Eugenie lifted the black mantilla from her hair. As it dropped, she felt naked, but his gasp of recognition eased the first of her many worries. The black lace had disguised her from Groningen to here. "Good afternoon, Sir Roger."

"Madame de la Croix. We thought you lost to us."

"I nearly was. And I am she no longer. Please to remember that."

Nazenby was much as she remembered him: a slim man, well-dressed in the height of English fashion. His striped waistcoat and bright yellow ascot drew attention from his features. His legendary sartorial elegance disguised his lethality better than her lacy veil and heavy cloak disguised her identity. Hiding her appearance, though, kept her alive.

"Come, sit down." He gestured with a pale-skinned hand. "Would you care for wine?"

"Cognac, if you have it."

That request startled the great man. After a hesitation, he did not deny her the stronger liquor usually reserved for men. She crossed to the marble-wrapped hearth, empty of fuel in London's summer. Throwing open her cloak, she took the closer seat and eyed the great spycatcher.

He had not greatly changed in nine years: more grey hairs peppered his hair, but his back remained stiff and straight. A few more lines on his face, but nothing that marred his elegance. Eugenie had timed her arrival to intercept him before any evening's entertainment. He looked almost the same as he had upon their first meeting in Paris, only a few months after she'd ventured to the capitol to locate her missing brother. Her masquerade as the wife of Louis Langlais de la Croix had temporarily fooled even the keen-witted Nazenby.

Her own mirror revealed how much she herself had changed. Six years of deprivation had sucked the fat silkiness from her flesh. She had no silver yet, but weary hollows darkened her skin. In Paris, she had attired beautifully, as befitted the rich widow of *M'sieur de la Croix*. When she fled, she had dressed to hide. Everything that remained to her, including her dull green traveling gown, was travel-worn and out of fashion.

Nazenby handed her a snifter. She glanced up as she accepted it and caught his narrowed eyes. "Counting the changes, Sir Roger?"

"I do apologize."

She shrugged. "Do not. I myself have counted each one. As I count your changes."

A smile flickered out at her honesty, then he gave her an unexpected compliment. "You speak English with only a slight accent now."

She watched the cognac swirl in the glass. "That is not the greatest change."

"No, it is not. I must say, your name was not one that I ever expected to hear." He leaned back on his upholstered chair, but remained stiff. "You were reported arrested. Executed within the week. How did you escape?"

"And who died in my place?" she added softly. Her lashes lifted. *Yes,* she watched him closely, *that was his chief question. Not how I escaped, but who was sacrificed to enable my escape.* "Here is a name for your dossier: Annette DesChamps. My cousin from Saumer died in my place. The authorities did not realize their mistake. She must have screamed of their mistake, but why would they believe any prisoner who matched the description of the woman they needed to arrest?

Annette and I did look much alike."

"How did she fall into their trap?"

"Whoever in my household betrayed me did not know that she had arrived late the night before."

"You were ... fortunate."

Eugenie's eyelids flared. "I still am. I still bear the guilt of her death. Do not think, Sir Roger, that I am blithe and carefree. Her death by the greatest of misfortunes aided my escape. She remains on my conscience."

He did not pursue a dialogue about Annette. He sipped his cognac then asked again, "How did you escape?"

Eugenie had known she must reveal much to the Englishman before he would help her. "Madame de la Croix would have fled west or north. I went to Metz, to an old friend of Louis, a man unknown to his associates in Paris."

He followed what she had buried in the list of places. "Louis told you of Abbé Villiers?"

"The abbé helped me travel to Brussels."

"You risked his life. He is a great contact for us."

"Never fear that I was in a foolish headlong flight."

"You should not have risked him. Louis Langley would have taught you that."

"I took great care, Sir Roger. I approached him in the church confessional. I took only information from him. We were never seen together. This is the training of Louis, to protect this back door from France. Was the abbé taken up?"

"He was not."

"*Alors*," the word escaped with her relief. "I am reassured, as you doubtless are. Poulaine would have been a dog after his bone, snatching anyone up since his two objects escaped him, myself and Delaney."

"How do you know Delaney escaped?"

"I encountered an associate of his in Dusseldorf. Only he used Delaney's other alias, Jean Louis Jettere."

"So, Paris to Metz, and Metz to Brussels." He sipped his cognac again. His crossed leg swung, the buckle on his polished shoe flashing in the dreary daylight. "From Brussels to Dusseldorf, I must presume, since you encountered one of Delaney's contacts there. And then to where, Madam?"

"Groningen."

"An unusual choice."

"The very reason I chose it. But it is not easy to sell jewels for their worth in that city." Remembering the dark streets where she had hidden while she slaved at work, she shivered. She sipped the cognac in her turn, and it warmed her core. "Earning the money for my passage from Groningen to Dover took much time. You English have many smugglers plying the waters of the Channel. They care not at all whom they ferry to their home shores as long as one pays the exorbitant price."

"You are recently arrived in England?"

"Very recently. I come to you first."

"You wish me to give you Delaney's identity?"

"Delaney? No. I do not wish to know it. Such knowledge is dangerous, for me, for him. Poulaine will still be on the hunt. Six years will not have slackened his pursuit. He is a man who does not forget."

"He thinks you dead."

"Do not make the mistake that others have with Didier Poulaine, Sir Roger. He never, never forgets an enemy. He will end his hunt only when he has found his prey or when he dies."

"He thinks you are dead."

Eugenie continued to shake her head. "Poulaine would have known the mistake of Annette's arrest as soon as he returned to Paris. He is a man who would not care that he sacrificed her. For this reason alone I have never returned to France."

"You must miss your home," he said blandly.

She narrowed her eyes then quickly smoothed away the revealing expression. "France has not been my home for many years. I am no *Bonapartiste*. Louis told you that."

"He never explained the reason you married him. I know before his death that you ran his messages and ferreted out information. That was the only reason I consented to Ken—Keiran Delaney's association with you."

He thought her a traitor to Louis' ideals and work in Paris. After six years and her life in jeopardy, he still thought she had sold Delaney out to the French spymaster Poulaine. "I am no double agent. I was not the reason that Poulaine identified us as spies."

"Perhaps," he allowed, and her frustration increased. "I will want to talk with you more on that matter."

"I do not support the current French regime. Louis told you this."

"I admit that Louis never fully explained the reason you hated Boney."

Eugenie's hand shook. She set the snifter on a side table, but she knew Nazenby had spotted that betraying tremor. "Napoleon killed all the men of my family, Sir Roger. My older brother was one of the sick at Acre that Napoleon poisoned before his retreat. His consul exiled my father to French Guiana. Papa did not survive the voyage. My younger brother was abandoned, alone in Paris, when my father was arrested. He must have been murdered or left to die. That is a better ending than others that I have imagined. Rainier was only eight, Sir Roger, and recovering from an illness when my father was arrested." After ten years, her anger still burned like acid. "When I reached Paris, the concierge of Papa's hotel could only tell me that Rainier had disappeared the night Papa was arrested. He had only eight years. Eight." She dashed away angry tears.

"You were not much older, were you? Louis told me you were twenty when he married you. That was a lie, wasn't it?"

"He believed the age I told him."

"How old?"

"What does it matter?" Sudden weariness slumped her shoulders. The sips of cognac had lost their bracing effect, and she shivered with a soul-deep chill. "I had five and ten years. But Louis, he did not consummate the marriage. He told you this. I heard him."

"He did. Do you think your vehement hatred of Napoleon is born of your youth? Many countries make mistakes."

"*Oui, c'est vrai.* But Napoleon is power-mad and manipulative. I warned Louis of this. I warned him that Napoleon wanted all of Europe. Has that not come true? England remains the only hope to stop him, so I throw my lot in with you."

Her tirade affected him not at all. "Throw your lot in with us? You picked up some gambling cant in your travels, didn't you?"

"I learned the most of it from your Keiran Delaney. He was as reckless as a gambler at the tables, with his *jeu parti.*"

Nazenby set aside his snifter. "What do you want, *Mdm. de la Croix?*"

"I have said: I am no longer she. She was a mask for a time and a place. I have been many names in the past six years. I would return to being myself."

Resting his elbows on the chair arms, he templed his fingers. "And who is that?"

"Ah no, Sir Roger. To return to myself, I must be assured of safety. Louis warned me about you. Once you have a spy, you never release him. But I will not spy for you. I cannot any longer. Not in Paris. Not anywhere that Bonaparte controls. The world has narrowed for me."

"I repeat: what do you want?"

"Louis left me money in your English bank—unless you consider his coin belongs to your government."

"Louis funded his own mission, *Madame.* That enabled him to ignore my advice."

Eugenie lifted one eyebrow, for Sir Roger had advised Louis to distance himself from the young *Française* who pretended to be his wife. She did not task him with that, though. "And the Langley family?" she asked, revealing that she knew de la Croix was an assumed name.

Sir Roger dropped his hands. He continued to swing one elegantly hosed leg. "He had no heirs. His money was his own. If he bequeathed it to you, it remains yours, even after nine years."

His words tallied with what Louis had told her in the days before his body failed. "You ask what I want? I wish a place, a place to live much retired."

"You are still young. You are as beautiful and elegant as ever, Madame. Finding another protector would not be difficult. I can introduce you—."

"*Non. Sacre bleu*, you misunderstand. I will not live in London. I wish a *petite maison* in the country. *Mon famille*, we had a farm before my father involved himself in the politics of the Republic. I wish such a place to find."

"My home is in London, not the country."

"*Tiens*, again you misunderstand. Is this with deliberation? I do not involve you, Sir Roger. I tell you. I will find my little house. You need not lift a finger."

"Then why are you here?"

"Me, I know you, the great spycatcher of England. It is a hunt for you. I come here this day, for very soon you will hear of a French widow, residing in England. You will suspect her. You keep a finger tracking all the *émigrés*, this you must do. If you hear of such a *Française*, with such-and-such a name, you would send one of your people to investigate. And you would speculate on my intentions. So I tell you now, whether you believe me or not.

"I do not return to the spy game and work against you. I am no *Bonapartiste*. You never trusted me, not as Louis and Delaney did. I come here and tell you all this. You will continue to doubt me; it is your way. Louis told me this. *Mais si*, you will know where I live, for I will write to you a letter for that purpose." Eugenie leaned back and took a deep breath. She gave him her wide guileless eyes and knew he would still doubt. "I will do all this with your consent."

Nazenby leaned forward. "Why do you need my consent? You have no connection to me. You never worked for the British government. Your plan is in motion."

"It is not a plan, not as Louis and Delaney would make the plans to get the information you wanted. I wish only to live a quiet life in your English countryside. Me, I am practical, for the great Sir Roger Nazenby would be very suspicious if I did not apprise you of this beforehand. Would you not?"

"I find myself suspicious because you inform me of your plans."

Eugenie dipped her head and picked up the brandy snifter. "This is as it should be. I played a double game in Paris, did I not? You would be a fool to trust me now. You will keep a watch upon me. I wish you to do so."

His mouth twitched. "A useless watch when you know my man is there."

"Whether I know or not, I will always anticipate that he is. Always."

"You are as suspicious as I am."

She sipped the cognac. "It is how I stayed alive, Sir Roger. Not all in my household did. My innocent cousin suffered and died. And I never could discover if Delaney knew I had escaped."

"You wish to be re-united with him?"

"*Non!*"

"He reported you dead. He saw you executed."

"The fool! He should not have returned to Paris."

"Should I inform Ken-Keiran Delaney that you survived and are in England?"

"To what purpose? To weigh him down with guilt? No. He could not save Annette. He should not have tried to save me."

"Will you seek him out?"

She laughed, brief and humorless. "We were not lovers. Poulaine thought we were. Did you think that as well, Sir Roger?"

"He gave the impression of a man enamored of you. If you expect to find him, he's not the man you will remember. He's hardened. He's earned a reputation as a rake and a gamester, and he deserves it."

"I do not wish to find him. I do not seek that old life. It is gone, as cold as my mother and my father, my brothers and my cousin Annette, all in the grave. That life is over. Not to be forgotten, but also not to be re-lived." She set aside the scarcely sipped cognac and lifted the mantilla over her head as she rose.

Ever the gentleman, Nazenby rose as well. "You have a direction for me?"

"No." She smiled. A little of her natural humor, repressed throughout this interview, peeked through. "For I did not know if my plan could continue. I do live on your graces, Sir Roger."

"A quiet country life." He shook his head. "You will find that dull after your adventures."

Eugenie laughed. "I will find it very far from dull."

Chapter 1 ~ Monday, 24 February 1812

Little Houghton, Yorkshire

Eugenie caught the hands of the little boy and spun him round and round until she staggered. Laughing, they both fell onto the rain-damp ground.

An older boy plopped down beside her. "I like it here best, Mrs. DesChamps."

"Because I do not give you the chores and make you study your lessons, yes? Escape, it is necessary, Matthew. It does not always last as long as we want, though." *Two years, not nearly long enough*, and Eugenie prayed that her little sanctuary would continue to last.

A shadow fell over them. A frisson of alarm running over her, Eugenie blinked, but the person blocking the sunlight was only Matthew's sister Melly Ratcliffe.

"You'll get damp on the ground. It was hard frost this morning and frost on the morrow. Up with you three."

"See?" she said to the boys. "Responsibilities crowd at us." But she stood and brushed over her backside. Her skirt was damp. "Hot tea, Melly?"

"Piping hot." The young woman smiled. "With scones," she directed at the boys. They yelped and ran for the house. "Scones are only for boys who wash their hands and faces," she called after them.

Without turning around, Matthew waved at his sister. He said something to the smaller boy, and their speed to the house picked up.

Melly laughed and linked her arm with Eugenie. "Mention food, and boys lose all manners. You have charmed another one, Eugenie."

"What? Little Robert? How is this? Does no one else spin him in the air? I do not believe it. And he likes scones more than he likes me. Both of them do. Men will always want food over women."

"You are no romantic."

She chuckled. "Me, I am practical."

They reached the garden gate that the boys had left open. Eugenie *tsked* and let Melly precede her. She shut it firmly then turned and realized that the younger woman was not only waiting, but she looked determined about something.

"You have news, I think."

"How do you do that, Jenny? Sometimes I think you are a witch. I know you are. Yes, I have news. He's coming."

"He is? Your Mr. Kennit? Has he written? Melly, my sweet friend, you will be married before Pentecost, if not before."

"My father will not want us to marry so soon. He will think it ill-advised."

"Then you and your Mr. Kennit must convince him otherwise. You must enlist your mother and your great-aunt. When does he arrive? What will you wear? Come, we have plans to make. I do not like this fashion of damp petticoats. I will succumb to a catarrh and miss Mr. Kennit's arrival."

Melly glanced at her back. "It's not just your petticoats that are damp." Giggling, they entered the house.

Watching her friend and the two boys consume hot tea and scones and the little savory tarts, Eugenie realized that she would soon lose her friend to this Mr. Kennit with his farm in Wales and a house in London. She did not want her to marry, but she knew Melly considered herself in love with Tobias Kennit. If the Rev. Ratcliffe approved of his daughter's choice, what right did she, an outsider hiding in Little Houghton, have to interfere in the marriage? And her interference would be for selfish reasons. No, she would say nothing.

She would miss Melly. The young woman and her brother brought laughter to Eugenie's *petite maison* nearly on a daily basis. Such brightness kept the shadows of the past at bay.

She did not know that soon those shadows would step once more into the light.

. ~ . ~ . ~ .

Monday, 24 February 1812 ~ London

Tobias Kennit saw Sir Roger Nazenby enter the Straights' main gaming room. The man looked neither left nor right but headed immediately for the card tables where Toby sat.

He ground his teeth. The old spycatcher obviously had tracked him here. *What game does Sir Roger hope to lure me into?*

Nazenby had the grace to move among the tables. Only those who watched closely would realize his focus was Kennit. He waited to approach the table until the last trick was tallied. As his partner congratulated Toby and they gathered up their winnings, Nazenby separated from the onlookers and closed the distance.

"A well-played game," he offered.

Toby didn't look up. His partner grinned. "We did trounce them." Distracted by a waving friend across the room, he excused himself and moved off.

Nazenby took another step closer. "I am gratified to find you returned to London."

He looked up then, his eyes narrowed. "A flying visit. I'm on my way north."

"To propose to your vicar's daughter?"

Toby knew that the old spycatcher still kept a map pin to mark all his spies, active or not, but he hadn't realized his personal map pin had remained so up-to-date. He'd been out of the spy game for eight years, since the debacle that ended in the execution of his remaining ally in Paris. "When will you release me, Sir Roger? When will you burn that file on me?"

The man smiled. He nodded to a man nearby, surveyed the gaming room, then began moving with Toby. "I thought I had let one person go, but I find two strings still attached. Your vicar's daughter lives in Little Houghton, doesn't she?"

"Not once I convince her father that I am worthy of her."

"Hence the weeks at your home in Wales, determining your assets and restoring your manor to a glory that your bride will find acceptable."

Toby scowled. He didn't care who saw his displeasure with Nazenby. "What bush are you beating around? I won't delay my journey for you. I quit working for you in `04."

"Yes. I remember that tirade very well. I have my carriage. I can return you to your *pied à terre* or take you on to your next evening's entertainment."

He wanted to glare and protest that he wasn't ready to leave Straights, but he'd decided a half-hour ago that he was bored with the level of competition. He missed Gordon Musgrove. He missed pitting his wits against Josette Sourantine. He missed Melly outwitting him at a simple game of Speculation. All three of them were better opponents than the men he'd played against tonight.

"Home for me," he said. Since he knew Nazenby wouldn't talk in a public place, he added, "I'm grateful for the offer of the carriage ride. It may be late February, but it's blasted cold."

The porter held their coats. Toby shrugged into his greatcoat while a footman assisted the older man with his. Then they entered the frigid night and strode down the street to the waiting carriage. The restless horses jingled their harness. Their breaths fogged in the cold air. The two men settled in the carriage. Nazenby knocked on the roof with his cane, and it rolled forward smoothly.

A streetlamp flashed its light into the carriage, illuminating a frown on the older man's face. Toby didn't like that look. The old spycatcher would try to manipulate him into a simple little assignment then the next one and then a third, and before he knew how, he would find himself back on the continent.

He crossed his arms over his chest and braced against the sway of the carriage. "It's been eight years, Nazenby, yet here you come. Again. My answer is the same. I won't work for you."

"I do not ask you to throw your lot back into the spy game, Kennit. As someone once told me, the spying world narrowed for you when you were nearly arrested in Paris." He paused, and another streetlamp revealed his frown. "I want—I need two things. Rumors are circulating that more French agents have entered England, looking for particular agents of ours who were once active in France. I wish to warn you of that."

"Is this related to that Sourantine woman?"

"No, we arrested her puppetmaster, Robert LeBrun. He's traveled on to a hotter place. Claude Thierry remains imprisoned. I wished to have him shipped to Calais in the middle of the night. And for him to have a very rough crossing. That is not yet to be."

"Could another spymaster have taken control have returned? Josette—Lady Hargreaves will be in danger if he did."

"I warned Hargreaves to have a special care for his wife. A new spymaster is always a danger. Most of Thierry's agents are known to us now, and we can keep a constant watch. That makes them useless to the French."

"Useless in London, not in York or Scotland or Ireland."

Nazenby lifted his upper lip. "No known agent has entered those places. Not yet."

Toby supposed the spycatcher didn't need his advice. The carriage started around a turn, and he braced against it. He thought of that spidery web that LeBrun and Thierry had controlled. The removal of those two and the death in a carriage accident of one of their chief agents had crippled the web of French spies in London and south England. Toby knew, from his own experience, that a crippled web could be revived. He'd helped Louis Langley revive the English web in Paris. He had never learned who remained after he fled and Louis' French wife was executed. Asking about active agents put them in danger. Toby had barely escaped arrest and execution. He wouldn't jeopardize anyone who remained in the spying game, a dangerous game, like Roulette, which he refused to play.

"And the rest of the French agents? How many of those did LeBrun sacrifice?"

"Not as many as I had hoped for. Whoever replaced him, however, came into a crippled operation."

"Or has crawled so deeply under rocks that you didn't even to think to look for them. But that doesn't concern me."

"It could concern you."

He shook his head before realizing that Nazenby wouldn't see it. The carriage had turned down a dark street, and the clouds blocked any moon shine. "No," he said sturdily. "It will not concern me. I'll keep an eye out for a murderous agent. You said *two things*. What is the second?"

"We have a cryptographer. His ciphers secure our communications to and from our various entities around the world. He lives in Little Houghton."

Toby grimaced. "Convenient for you."

"Very convenient. A few of the rumors have touched upon locating this man."

"Murder?"

"Kidnapping."

"Are they fools? A forced decryption of a cipher can be no more accurate than forced information."

"They seek more than decryption. Without his creation of new ciphers, the French would soon break all of our codes. Last Spring they tried a trap sweetened with a lovely lady. He enjoyed her attentions, but he kept careful guard on his work and his methods."

"Wise man."

"A very wise man. He clued me in to what was happening and mentioned it had happened the year before. Only then did we realize that a couple of men in the cipher department had fallen into the sticky trap. He also opened up several lines of enquiry that bore fruit. We are fortunate that the French did not identify him as the master that he is. He kept his true level of work hidden, and LeBrun never stumbled onto the truth."

"So they caught him, but he slipped off their hook long before they knew what a monster salmon they'd caught."

"Exactly. We have other cryptographers, but none with his talent. Taking this man away from us would cripple our efforts against Bonaparte."

"Murder is still their best alternative."

"Their second choice. What we have says, *Find him. Take him.* And we don't want to lose him." The carriage swayed as it turned. A streetlamp flashed its light into the carriage. Nazenby looked grim.

"You can put him into protective custody," Toby offered.

The old spycatcher grunted. "We tried that after the sweet spider's attempt. He refused to work at all until we released him. Our compromise was that he complete his work outside London with the knowledge that he would be under constant watch."

"How many on him?"

"Two of our best in his house, another in the village. And your contact—who will reveal himself at the appropriate time. You must connect with our cryptographer. I warn you: he may be obstreperous at first."

Toby had to grin. "This man and I could be friends. So, when I arrive in Little Houghton, what do you want me to do? Warn him?"

"I do not know if a warning will do any good. I have little personal acquaintance with him. He's in the military secrets branch. If a warning would alert him to defend himself, then that might be sufficient. If he is like the rest of that department, he won't know how to defend himself."

"Warn and protect."

"Watch and protect," Sir Roger clarified. The carriage halted. "Warn him only when you think it necessary."

"How will I determine when it is necessary?"

"You were in the game. You know." He rapped on the roof. The carriage swayed as a page jumped down to open the door and drop the step.

Toby gripped the door, holding it shut until he was ready to end this conversation. "You realize that I'll be distracted with my concerns. Please tell me you have someone else watching for French spies."

"Someone else—yes. You may recognize them, but that person may not offer any help."

"Look, Nazenby—."

"I will have another agent available in a fortnight. And the man has his own guards."

That sounded better. He released the door. As it opened, he asked, "Who is this great cryptographer?"

"Colonel Sir Charles Audley. Enjoy your visit to Little Houghton, Kennit."

Toby gave a derisive laugh.

.~.~.~.

Friday, 28 February 1812, Yorkshire

Charles Audley perched the pence-nez he didn't need on the end of his long nose.

He wished he'd never started this disguise as a bookish scholar who occasionally availed himself of the country pursuits of riding and shooting. He especially wished it when Eugenie DesChamps brought her *joie de vivre* into a room and yet seemed to ignore him out of all the others there.

He was the only bachelor; she, a young widow. The matchmakers had eyed them wistfully when he arrived in Little Houghton last fall. Intent on decrypting the newest French cipher, he had made the mistake of being too distracted the first three times they met. By the fourth, he had solved the problem, but her luminous eyes no longer settled on him.

She was a dark French beauty. If she hadn't already been settled in Little Houghton, he might have deemed her another sweet spider sent to steal his secrets and methods. The two men stationed in his manor had asked discreetly about her: a refugee who had settled in the village two years before. He didn't think the French would have such a long view, especially as they had learned of his work last winter, a full year after Eugenie DesChamps moved into his home village.

Since he had lifted his head out of that tricksy cipher, he had had opportunity to study his neighbors. None received as much of his attention as she did. Living in a small cottage, she employed only a maid and a man of all work. He heard she painted. Soft feminine watercolors, he'd guessed. After that fourth meeting, he twice tried to engage her in conversation. She hadn't snubbed him, but her short answers revealed she wanted to be elsewhere.

While he rapidly concluded that he wanted to be nowhere else except by her side.

He sighed and swirled the wine in his goblet and watched the Frenchwoman laugh with her friend Miss Ratcliffe. They spoke of the younger woman's return from London. Rumors of impending nuptials had surrounded the vicar's daughter. He hoped she would look for additional love matches to promote. She had caught him watching Madame DesChamps several times. Thus far, she had done nothing. He could use the plaguey matchmakers from his wild oats days.

What was the matter with young women these days? Didn't they want their friends as happy as they were?

He would have to make the move soon before other bachelors and widowers decided Madame DesChamps would make a cozy addition to their nests. *How did no one scoop her up before I came to Little Houghton?*

Ryland Cable, host of this evening, walked over to him. "You've been looking at her since October. You need wings on those feet, Audley."

He groaned. "Am I that obvious that even you have noticed?

"Even me. I'm not blind. Although I didn't see it until my wife pointed it out at last Sunday's service. She said you needed a push. I came to give it."

"Tonight? No. She's talking to Miss Ratcliffe."

"She always talks to Melly Ratcliffe. If you go over there and Melly doesn't back off, I'll fetch her off myself. Now go, man."

Charles drained his wine and set the glass on the table. He lifted his chin over the stiffly starched points of his collar. He rolled his shoulders.

Cable clapped a hand on his back. "Go on now."

He felt the eyes on him as he crossed the room. Miss Ratcliffe saw him coming and murmured to Mdm. DesChamps. The widow's back stiffened. Then she said something that elicited a giggle from her friend. By then, Charles had reached them. He thought about going on past the two women—but he had wasted his opportunities last October and November because he'd been too abstracted with his work to notice anything not under his nose. Even the cook had learned to place a plate in front of him to get him to eat.

He took the necessary sidestep and stopped at her right elbow, so close that she could jab him if he insulted her. As he likely would. His foot had been known to insert itself into his mouth.

Miss Ratcliffe dipped an abbreviated curtsey. With a murmur she faded away.

And he stood side by side with Mdm. DesChamps, both of them with their backs to the watching room.

"Madame DesChamps, how are you this evening?"

"I find it cold. And you, Colonel Audley?"

She had trouble with the military rank, pronouncing all the vowels, but he didn't feel sure enough of himself to correct her. "I am fine." More words failed him. He knew he should ask something. *What? Maybe a compliment.* Her golden gown did wonders for her. Not many women could carry off such a color. He liked the way the gown fit her body, especially her ... chest. He probably shouldn't mention that. *No, Charles old chap, stay away from all talk about her gown.*

The shoulder nearest him gave a tiny hitch. "*Fine.* This is one English word that I find fascinating. You English say it whether you are in good spirits or have the megrims. That is the word, *n'est ce-pas*, megrims? And *fine*? The weather, it is *fine*. The road from London, it is *fine*. The vicar's sermon—."

"Not *fine*," he leaped in. "Perhaps this week's text should have been a New Testament verse on Love thy Neighbor."

She half-turned, and Charles matched her, careful not to overstep that slight turn. "Or a parable," she countered. "The Parable of the Prodigal Son, a man who wasted his opportunities. That would have been my choice."

This woman had a sharp dagger to point at him. He started to enjoy this conversation. "Perhaps not the profligate prodigal. Something from the Sermon on the Mount. Blessed are the Peacemakers or Faith as Strong as a Mustard Seed. Faith that Moves Mountains," he added, his brain tossing up sermon titles."

"Faith that Moves Mountains?" She turned fully toward him and lifted her gaze. "I am accounted tall for a woman, but *vraiment*, I am not so big as a mountain." She looked down her form, luscious in the golden silk with its white lace squaring the neckline.

"No, not you, personally. Your stubbornness—."

"And now I am stubborn."

He removed the pence-nez. "I have stuck my foot in my mouth."

She gave a ripple of laughter. "I find that a delightful image, Col. Audley. Your idioms are sometimes incomprehensible, but I understand that one very well."

Honesty appeared to work quite well. As long as he stayed away from her gown. "I have stuck my foot in my mouth since our first meeting, Mdm. DesChamps. I had a tricksome problem that consumed me, and when I looked up from it, you had flitted away."

"*Non, non*, Colonel. You cannot call me a mountain and then say that I flitted away. No mountain can flit."

"Both feet," he said morosely.

She laughed. She must have taken pity on him, for she patted his arm then left her hand resting on the black superfine of his coat. "Come, we must find a subject that does not leave you with both feet in the mouth. For example, I must always wonder the reason you say *Mdm. DesChamps* when others merely say *Mrs. Deschamps*." She gave the different pronunciations without hesitation. "Have you a reason to remind yourself that I am French?"

She hid her cleverness with charm. Two displays of intelligence in less than a minute. That snared him as completely as her beauty did. Now, how to keep her by his side? *In with both feet*, he reminded himself. "I thought—I hoped using the French pronunciation would bring home back to you. You must miss France. When did you come over?"

She withdrew a little, slipping her hand from his arm. "I became no longer a Frenchwoman with the Revolution, Colonel. England is my home now. I would ask that you no longer remind me of the lost past, as far from me as the *ancien regime* is from the rule of France."

"Forgive me. I do keep blundering about. Perhaps we should talk of things not personal. This landscape, for example. It is a new addition to Mr. Cable's collection. I like it."

Her chuckle was muted but real, and his heart leapt at the sound. "You like it? As do I. Tell me what you like most about it."

Eager to remove a foot from his mouth, Charles scrambled for an answer. "The smooth undulation of the land while turbulent clouds cover the sky. The colors of the heather juxtaposed against the range of stormy greys. That single opening of the clouds, sending a shaft of light onto that tree. I've seen that happen on the moors. And I know this place, just not that lone tree. I've walked across that upland many times. There's no trees, not a stand, not even one."

"The artist's insertion. Do you think the tree is a needless addition?"

He wondered at that question, then he began to suspect the artist's identity. "Not needless. Gives us a focus, doesn't it? With the light shining on it."

"Then you think it necessary?"

"I like how the tree limbs are bending to the wind. Not giving up, taking another way. We have to do that in life. Not give up, not give in. Find another way."

Over the top of her wine glass she gave him an approving smile. "Has Col. Charles Audley had to find another way? I thought him one of the privileged."

He could drown in those dark eyes. He forced himself to look at the landscape. "I've had to find another way more times than I can count on both hands. I'm not so privileged, Madame. I've been that tree, storms over me, alone in the world." He glanced at her. Her gaze was lifted to the painting, but she seemed to look far beyond this room, perhaps even this England. How many times had she had to find another way? "Do you know the artist? I would pay well for a landscape of this quality."

Her attention came back to him. "Truly? I might be able to arrange a meeting between you and the painter."

He wanted to draw her out, so he tempted her to reveal her secret with "Give the fellow his due. Call him the artist he is."

"And if he is a she?"

"I'll still call her an artist. That scrawl in the bottom right, that's you?" He stepped up to the mantel and lifted his pence-nez to read. "E. DesChamps. Definitely you." As he came back, he noticed the many gazes turned to watch them. He tucked the spectacles in his vest pocket and hoped she did not think him old because he'd used them.

Eugenie did not remark on the pence-nez, and she seemed unconcerned with the room behind them. "You are not shocked that I mess with the oils when I should be managing a household. Many men would be."

"I've seen your household. I'd be surprised if you ever need more than a girl and a handyman. You're too talented with the oils to give up painting."

"I am gratified that you are not shocked. And I bask in your praise."

"That painting deserves praise. You deserve praise for coming out with it."

Eugenie shook her head. "It is hard to judge one's own work. I have a certain satisfaction when I complete a piece, you understand, but how will others judge my work? They offers compliments, but are they truthful?"

"You have other canvasses?"

"Very few here. I have sent a few small canvasses to a gallery in London. The owner does not wish the patrons to know the artist is a mere female."

"Thus, the signature *E. DesChamps*. Does your gallery owner know you're female?"

"He does. It was his decision to keep my gender unknown."

"I hope you're making a pretty pile of guineas with him."

"Not quite a pile, but enough to supplement my wants as well as my needs. Mr. Faulkner, he wishes me to give him a large landscape such as this one, but Mr. Cable demanded this one as soon as he saw it."

Jealousy raised its ugly head. "When did Cable see it?"

"When his wife and he came to pick up the small oils of their children. Those hang in the entrance hall. Did you see them?"

He remembered the light-gilded oval portraits hanging at the foot of the staircase. They had attracted his eye, but he had given them only a passing glance. "A different style."

"Children should be soft and fresh. Were I skilled at watercolors I would have attempted that medium. Instead, I contended with a light palette and a lighter hand. I must confess, I do enjoy the starker, heavier landscapes. Children's portraits are my bread and butter, though."

He had lifted his gaze back to the painting. "What did you call it? Don't artists name their works?"

"*Un Reve de Paix.*"

"*Dream of Peace*," he translated softly. He could not remember what painting had previously hung above the mantel. Maybe a stuffy ancestor. "Yes. All the storminess of the clouds, but there, a shaft of sunlight on that patch of green tree. A bit of blue in the swirls of heavy greys. I like that title." He looked at her as he gave the compliment and saw a pleased smile curving her mouth.

"*M'sieur* Cable did not like it. Nor did his wife. They call it *Storm over the Moor*."

"Your title is better."

That pleased her, for her hand returned to his arm. "You are not just being polite, Col. Audley?"

"Have you not seen multiple evidences of my lack of diplomacy, Mdm. DesChamps?"

She chuckled. "True. Very true."

He was winning this battle, even after insertion of both feet. Honesty served him well with this woman. *How can I find a way to increase our time together?* "Have you always painted?"

"Circumstances forced me to abandon it for a few years. Never the sketching. That was sometimes a little money-maker. I have made a tidy little sum with the portraits, especially General Reinholt's wife, but I do not like the portraits."

Her accent thickened a little when she talked rapidly, as she did recounting the first oils she attempted after moving here.

When she slowed down, he had his next question ready. "Where do you paint? This," he motioned to *Un Reve de Paix*, "was not done in the *plein aire*."

"No. The sketch was. Several sketches actually, before it all came together. I do paint where I have a view of the moor. I converted the sitting room into my studio. When you visit me, Col. Audley, do not raise your English nose at taking tea in the little room that should be the dining room."

"Am I invited for tea?"

"But, of course. We will have little tarts both savory and sweet. I am also good with pastry, but my cook, she is a genius with the fillings."

Charles began to breathe a little easier. He had not wanted to push too fast, too hard, especially since he had barely recovered the ground he had lost. Yet he wanted a relationship not dependent on Sunday sermons and dinner parties hosted by their neighbors. A visit over tea sounded a good start.

"And after we have tea and you have shown me your studio, I would commission a landscape from you, Mdm. DesChamps. A painting of the moors behind Ridings, with the spring sun greening the fields and the high moors untamed behind cultivated fields. Or better yet, the moors from my study window." If she sketched while he worked in his study—or if he could convince her to work at Ridings, he would have the uninterrupted time to court her.

Eugenie gave him quite a different look. He might call that gleam in her eye mercenary. "You may not want a landscape when you hear what I will charge."

With a recklessness not like him, he said, "I want that painting by you, no matter the expense."

Her long lashes flickered. "*Non*, you must not say that. You make me wish to be greedy. The autumn and Noël cost more than I had anticipated. When will you come to tea? Tuesday? Thursday?"

He wanted to say tomorrow, but he took the hint that she might not be ready for visitors on Monday. Nor did he want to seem over-eager, just eager enough. "Will Wednesday suit you? I have a prior commitment on Tuesday."

"Wednesday it is." She presented her silk-gloved hand, as if they were striking a business deal.

He took it, wishing he palmed her flesh rather than white silk that matched her gown's trimmings. And he held her hand longer than necessary for a business deal. "Am I now invited into the realm of friendship?"

An eyebrow lifted. "Are we not all friends in Little Houghton?"

"Then I may call you Eugenie when we need not be formal? As we must be here."

"Many here call me Jenny."

"Eugenie is too pretty to be reduced to that."

She blushed, surprising him. She had faced off with him, accepted his blunders, heard his compliments of her art, but a compliment to her name brought pleased color to her cheeks. "I like that you give it the French pronunciation. Yes, you have leave to call me by my true name, if I may call you—." She paused, letting him give her his name.

"Charles," he quickly supplied. When she repeated it, softening the *ch*, every part of him tightened.

Chapter 2 ~ Friday, 28 February 1812

London

Didier Poulaine waited although he did not like to wait. He hid his impatience with the skill of many years. He knew when to tighten the strangling knot and when to release it. He knew when to slip the dagger in. He knew when to sit back and let the world stream by. After years in the business, he knew the world would offer up the proper opportunity.

This opportunity, for example. An opportunity that he had thought missed. On a mission to capture the master cryptographer for the English, he heard a name that he had not heard for eight years. *Keiran Delaney.* A pretend Irishman who had masqueraded as the French officer Jean Louis Jettere. The *Anglais* Delaney had slipped the noose in `04 along with another double agent. Two operatives who escaped him. Over the years, Poulaine made doubly sure no other escaped.

Delaney's name had dropped in connection with finding another Military Secrets informant.

The information had slipped through the stream and found him. Here, in London, he would finally have his chance. To hold a slender dagger to the man's neck, to feel and smell the terror engendered by the prick of that steel blade—that would appease his long unslaked anger.

It could be a trick. Poulaine knew that. A ruse to draw out more French agents for capture. Jacques Saultsein had warned him before Poulaine shipped across the Channel. The English spycatcher was on an active hunt for French agents. They had lost several well-placed spies and their best informant. Finding a replacement who had direct White Hall access would be difficult—which was one reason this *Anglais* could be a trap.

Poulaine hadn't acted on the information. He waited. Confirmation was needed. Who better to find it for him than Saultsein, the new French spymaster in London? He had ventured to the address given to him. Then he set up a watch, to see who entered the new spymaster's house. Caution meant life.

When the soft rain started, he'd left his post watching the house and entered this gallery. He did not think he'd been spotted. He wasn't certain who waited for him there. His informant offered no particulars, only that contact was possible. The suave courier had known nothing of his replacement except this address. Poulaine would wait and watch before he contacted the man. Two days was not so long when measured against eight years.

And in waiting he'd again heard Delaney's name, spoken by two men swilling beer in a pub. Foolish men. He had tracked one of them back to his lodgings. If nothing came of his meeting with the new spymaster, he would visit that man. In the deeps of the night, no one would hear muffled screams.

He smiled to himself.

A carriage rumbled past. He looked out the window, but the carriage did not halt at the house he watched.

"Sir." An effete young man, willowy rather than sturdy English oak, approached him. "May I help you, sir? Has that painting attracted your attention?"

Poulaine stared down his long nose at the assistant then looked at the painting before him.

"One of our exclusive artists. This is *Wild Moor*," the assistant said.

"This is typically English."

"Yes, sir. The Yorkshire moors. I myself have never ventured to those hinterlands. Do I detect a French accent, sir?"

"I was born in France," he allowed.

"You fled the Revolution, Monsieur?" He butchered the appellation although he seemed proud to know the French word. "We do have a few paintings of French scenes. One might strike your eye."

The gallery's assistant pointed out a light-capturing oil of the Pantheon atop Sainte-Genevieve hill. A heavy oil drew the lines of Notre Dame's two towers rising above the cathedral's roof. A sketch of the Louvre's colonnade. A few street scenes. Poulaine liked none of them, but he followed the assistant to create the illusion of interest in art.

Then they came to a larger canvas of the French countryside.

Poulaine stopped. The sky above the farm had the brilliant blue it achieved only in October. Two figures had met in the golden wheat field. Bent stalks of grain revealed the path each had taken to meet. A meandering line of cedars marked the river. On the horizon were the clustered houses of a village, dominated by the Romanesque tower of a church.

"Ah, monsieur, you have a good eye. This is the same artist who painted *Wild Moor*, the canvas by the window that had your attention. This is definitely France."

Poulaine remembered that day. He remembered the blood on him after that meeting. And he remembered who had stood behind him on the hill.

For eight years he had looked for her. She had to be punished. She had turned against him after that day. She had not had the horror of staring at his bloody hands, but she must have watched. By no sign had she revealed that she saw him murder Etienne Foucault. She had chattered with ease all the way back to Paris. But she turned cool then icy.

He leaned closer to the painting but could not decipher the scrawled artist's name. "Who is the painter?"

The assistant did not have to look. "E. DesChamps."

DesChamps. Not de la Croix. But it had to be her. Or she had to have some connection to the artist.

The frail young man rattled on. "You will see the date is 1811. We received this canvas only a month ago. The artist was reluctant to part with it, but Mr. Rainsford was quite determined. He informed me that he demanded this canvas for the gallery. I see it has quite captured your interest."

"I like the style. And the light, that is very reminiscent of my childhood visits to the country. *Peut-etre*, is it that you have another canvas by this E. Deschamps?"

"No, only Wild Moor. DesChamps is brilliant with these small canvases. The interesting perspective! The quality of detail! I admit to you that we have difficulty keeping them in the gallery. I suspect *Wild Moor* will not last the month."

"But this one lingers. You said it arrived a month ago."

"That is correct. It is a larger canvas for this artist, which triples the price."

"I want it. And any other scene of France by E. DesChamps."

"Of course, monsieur. We currently have no such other canvas by DesChamps, but we have a fine watercolor of Avignon—."

"No. It is this DesChamps I am interested in. What information can you give me?" He almost added *about her*, but he didn't want the assistant to think he knew anything. *Is it Eugenie de la Croix, styling herself as E. DesChamps?*

"I know very little personally, monsieur."

"Your Mr. Rainsford. May I speak with him?"

"He is in the Lake District. I expect him to return by the end of next week. If you have a card—."

"No card. I will return next Friday."

"And will you wish this canvas, monsieur?"

"I will take it with me. Wrap it well." He produced his wallet and paid the amount the assistant named. Then he glanced back toward the window. "The *Wild Moor*. I am not certain that I will purchase that canvas, but it intrigues me. Would you place a *retainder* on it for me.

That is perhaps not the word."

"I think you may mean a retainer, a note that will hold the painting for you. Mr. Rainsford frowns upon that practice, monsieur."

"I do understand. Should another person wish to purchase the painting, you would be able to dissuade them, is it not so? For a small remuneration."

The young man's eyes gleamed. "Exactly so, monsieur. You name? And your residence? I will have the canvas sent—."

Poulaine dropped several guineas into the assistant's hand. "I will take it with me. My name is Chevalier. *Honoré de Chevalier*." He lied easily, from long practice, and the assistant never doubted him. He returned to the window to wait on the canvas.

Eugenie de la Croix, once his fascination, had become his enemy from the day of the wheat field scene she had painted. He had needed months to gather the evidence to convict her of spying for England and against her homeland. And when he moved to arrest the little spy-ring that circled around her, she had somehow evaded arrest.

DesChamps. E. DesChamps. Why did that name seem familiar?

His men had arrested the wrong woman. Poulaine had wasted days on the heels of his other quarry, the pretend Delaney. When he returned to Paris, his men reported their successful arrest. The error had not been discovered until he visited the Bastille.

His men had proudly displayed their captive. Swollen and mottled contusions had covered the woman's face and body. When he'd entered the cell, she remained collapsed on the filthy stones of her cell. He had snatched her hair and prepared to gloat over Madame Eugenie de la Croix. But something told him the captive was not the woman he needed to destroy. The coloring was right, hair and skin and eyes, what could be seen of them. She did not respond to his questions, to his shouts. She merely flinched when he slapped her. His men claimed that she had to be Mdm. de la Croix. He'd had his doubts.

Poulaine let the execution go forward then sought out the de la Croix house servants. Only from the upstairs maid did he learn that the cousin of Mdm. de la Croix had arrived late on the evening before the arrest. Another round of interviews with the servants uncovered little more. They knew only that she was called Annette and had arrived from Saumer.

To Saumer he had gone, but he could find no information about a Mdm. de la Croix.

"Monsieur." The gallery assistant irritated with his interruptions. "Your canvas. I wrapped it in paper and then oilcloth to protect it from the rain."

"*Merci*. You say the gallery owner—*zut alors*! I have forgotten his name," he lied.

"Rainsford. Geoffrey Rainsford. He returns on the sixth."

"*Bon, tres bon*. I will return the next day to discuss this artist with him."

He lifted the canvas and left the shop. Excitement raced in his veins, trembled in his muscles. Perhaps it was that Eugenie had shared her most vivid memory with an artist, someone from France, and he had painted it for her—only to have it refused. She would not want a scene of murder hanging in her home. Poulaine would track the artist, and the artist would give him Eugenie.

He needed to read the dossier he kept on the de la Croix woman and her associates, that Jean Louis Jettere and the Irishman Delaney. He had regretted not going with the soldiers to her residence, but he'd been after a bigger fish: the English agent.

Annette of Saumer. And now this artist E. DesChamps, who replicated on canvas that red day in October, the sun bright while the wind chilled. Somewhere he would find a connection to Eugenie de la Croix, and then he would have her. He would find her, and then he would kill her.

He would draw the knife across her throat himself.

But first he had a master cryptographer and a pretend Irishman to find.

Chapter 3 ~ Monday, 2 March 1812

Little Houghton

Toby let himself be led to the settle beside the fireplace. Young Matthew almost shoved him onto the bench. "My father will be here in a moment." Then the boy and his sister proceeded to stare at him.

Toby stared back. "And your sister?"

"She and Mama are visiting Mrs. DesChamps. They said they'd be back before tea."

"I see. When did you arrive back from London?"

"We've been back since Epiphany. Great-Aunt Cordelia was well enough by then," the girl announced.

Toby felt bad that he couldn't remember the girl's name, but he'd never made an effort to do so. It hadn't dawned on him to cozen up to the younger sister. Any time in that Eastcheap house that wasn't taken up by Melly had been confiscated by Matthew and his equally young cousin. He had obliged, but now realized his problem. "I am gladdened to hear that your aunt is improved."

"She's much better."

Matthew bounced on his toes. "Did you drive your carriage, Mr. Kennit?"

"I did."

"The high-stepping greys?"

Before Toby could answer, the sitting room door opened to reveal a lean man with a thinning head of hair as golden as his daughter was dark. Toby stood immediately and bowed, even as Matthew crowed, "That's Papa."

A bit of chaos as Matthew and his sister rushed to tell their father about Toby's arrival and Melly's location and their conversation. The girl looped an arm around his waist while Matthew hoarded the telling of minute details. When the boy eventually ran down, the vicar looked at his guest.

"You are patient, Mr. Kennit."

"I find patience wins a lot of battles."

"And even some wars?"

"I can only hope."

The vicar's eyes opened wider, revealing a color the same as his eldest daughter. Then they shuttered down, and Toby realized the man would be a fair opponent in any intellectual joust.

He unwrapped his daughter's arm. "I do think that I should have a few words alone with Mr. Kennit."

"Will he offer for Melly?"

"That is for him to say to me and not for you and your sister to speculate about. Off with you. Matthew, you have a Latin lesson to re-write before tea. And Miranda—."

She gave a heavy sigh. "I know. I am to write out a better copy of your letter to the bishop."

"This time, try to spell ecclesiastical correctly."

"Yes, Papa," and her brother echoed her. But Matthew sneaked a wink at Toby before he shut the door.

The Rev. Ratcliffe waited until the door shut before he extended a hand to Toby. "I apologize that my wife and I were not here to greet you."

"Young Matthew and—um, Miranda did a fine job. I was not bored once."

The vicar gave him a quizzical look. "I am not certain that is a good thing. But you are here now. Will you have tea? Or a mulled cider?"

"Cider sounds good."

He rang for the servant. The maid appeared quickly, apparently having waited in the hall. She curtsied on receiving the order for sherry and cider and disappeared.

"Did you have a good drive from London? You came in your curricle?"

"With my tiger behind me." Toby hid a grimace, and for the next quarter-hour pretended he was not bored with their conversation about the roads from London and the weather.

A commotion in the hallway broke through the talk of weather. Matthew and Miranda returned to the room. "Mama's back. And Melly," the boy added for Toby's benefit.

"Good, I will not have to bear the brunt of the entire conversation. But you, my son, have not finished that Latin lesson."

"I started the letter, Papa," the girl quickly added.

He smiled on her then frowned on his son. "Well?"

"If I finish it after tea, I will write an extra lesson tomorrow. May I stay for tea, Papa?"

He rolled his eyes heavenward. "I suppose I must since you are willing to sacrifice an extra hour of your day to Latin."

Matthew controlled a yelp of joy. Toby was not certain he would have been capable.

The boy perched on a chair. "Did you have to do Latin, Mr.

Kennit?"

"Latin and French and German at home, Greek when I went to Harrow, and all four with the addition of Italian at University."

"You have a knack for languages," Ratcliffe said.

"My mother is half-French, my father half-German. The extra languages were a necessity, they said. I found it helpful when I traveled on the continent."

"The Grand Tour?" Miranda asked, her blue eyes wide.

"Not quite," he hedged. He'd been masquerading his entire time in France and Germany. He had often yearned for an opportunity to speak English without worrying someone would overhear.

"No Portugal or Spain?" Matthew sounded disappointed.

"No time at all. No daring adventures with the army." He didn't even hint at his daring adventures as a spy. "I'm not a soldier."

The boy slumped, but the reverend nodded. "I spent a year in Italy, long before I met your mother," he added for the benefit of his children, "and enjoyed every moment of it. When I recounted my adventures, however, one of my friends said it sounded dull. I remember being fascinated every day."

"Did you have a favorite city, sir?"

"Florence," he said immediately. "Someday, when Napoleon is no longer rampaging, I hope to take my family there." He continued, describing the small villa on the city's outskirts and a few museums that had appealed to him. That served for conversation until the ladies joined them.

Toby bowed to Mrs. Ratcliffe. As that lady welcomed him, he smiled at Melly and was gladdened by her return smile. The maid brought in tea as his hostess disposed her family around the room, and he was gratified when Melly joined him on the settle.

"We have a little ritual, Mr. Kennit," the reverend said before reading out a passage from the Bible. "Miranda," he then prompted, and the girl explained about a mustard seed and how it came to be.

"And it's self-seeding," she added at the end. "If the seeds aren't collected, they'll drop to the ground and start new plants at the next growing season."

"That's an interesting point. If our faith is to be *as a mustard seed*, is it self-seeding?" With that question from the vicar, a lively conversation started up, young Matthew contributing as much as his sisters and parents did.

Toby stayed quiet, letting the words flow around him as he took a reading on the Ratcliffe family. The sandwiches and sweet pastries disappeared. The tea pot was emptied. His cider disappeared. He was stirred from his passivity by Matthew: "What do you think of mustard, Mr. Kennit?"

He cleared his throat. "I have always found that mustard goes very well with sausages."

"Oh, foul," Miranda said.

The vicar intervened. "Mr. Kennit did not come prepared for our debate. As arbiter, I declare his comment allowed and quite true." The hall clock chimed. "And tea is officially over." He came over to Toby, who quickly stood and took the man's extended hand. "Will you join us for dinner, Mr. Kennit? We keep country hours."

"I would be delighted, sir. Is there a lesson for the evening meal?"

"Lessons only at tea. I believe Melly wants to show you our garden, and from the hill you can see the village and the chief houses of the district."

"Wrap up well, Melly," her mother said. "Did you finish your Latin, Matthew?"

With a laughing look over her shoulder, Melly led him to the hall to collect their coats from the waiting footman. "Did you wait long for us to return?"

"A half-hour, I think. I wasn't marking the time. This is a pretty district."

Her violet eyes opened wide. Then she glanced at the footman. "I left on my boots in the hopes that Papa would want you to see the garden." Slipping a hand in the crook of his arm, she led him to the back of the house. "This way to the garden."

Toby admired the knot garden's design, looked at the plants beginning to send out green sprigs, and trailed his fingers through the rosemary to release its scent. At the foot of the garden they wound into a tree-lined lane with the moor at its end. "That's a hill," he said.

"Are you up for it?" she challenged.

They climbed the first upland slope before she called a halt. The wind blew stronger on the height, and Toby kept a watch for Melly's shivering, not wanting her to chill. "I'm game for more," he offered.

She shook her head. "I am not. Besides, if we climb higher, we'll miss dinner. Papa wanted me to show you the village and the houses. There." She turned him a little and pointed to the buildings clustered around a greystone church, its slate gleaming in the sunshine. "Little Houghton."

Moors surrounded the village, tucked in a lilliputian dale. A winding river sparkled in the sunlight, and the road snaked alongside it. Toby hadn't noticed the heights on his drive in, too concerned with reaching the inn before sundown. This morning he'd been aware of the uplands. Standing on this hillside, though, he realized the dominance of the moors.

"It's beautiful when the heather begins to bloom. Lovely colors. Purple and lilac and cherry pink. Occasionally you'll see white flowers. I do like the coppery color, but we don't usually see it here. You don't have moors in Wales, do you?"

"We have mountains. I live near Snowdon, in Gwynedd."

"That's one of the old kingdoms, isn't it? Long before the Saxons invaded England. I've been researching Wales, you see. You gave me very little information about your homeland."

"I didn't want to scare you off. Wales is ... remote."

Melly laughed. "Yorkshire is remote. And as long as I have the heights—*I will lift up mine eyes unto the hills*. Snowdon is the tallest mountain in Wales, isn't it?"

"The tallest mountain in Britain outside of the Scottish Highlands."

"I hear the Highlands are beautiful in summer."

"I hear they are even more remote."

She only smiled. "I am to tell you the major houses in the district. There, beside the village, is Mr. Cable's house."

"Red brick, three stories. I saw it on my drive in yesterday."

"Good. Look left, farther away. Newland. William Newland is the richest man in the district."

"I remember him. He's Josette's grandfather."

"Yes, and now look to the right, tucked against the moors. Ridings. Col. Charles Audley lives there."

Toby's ears perked up, although he strove to give no sign that he already knew that name. For a brief while he had forgotten Nazenby's mission for him: to watch and protect the cryptographer wanted by French agents. He would have to make an effort to meet the colonel.

He didn't know if the man would know Nazenby's name or not. He doubted it. The spycatcher had said the colonel was in one of the military departments. He'd also sounded skeptical of most of those men's abilities to defend themselves. A paper pusher, then, rather than an officer of the line. Good with ciphers meant he'd probably been immured in some university tower before the military tapped him on the shoulder. But all he said to Melly was "Mr. Cable in the red brick near the village. Ridings and Col. Audley by the moor."

"Yes. You can't see it, but there's a road running between the uplands. It goes all the way to Staithes, which is on the coast. Papa said it was an old smugglers' route. Mama said it goes much further back, to the Viking settlements. We were near Ridings today. My friend Mrs. DesChamps lives there. She is an artist."

"And the big house to our left, grey stone like the church. Who lives there?"

"The Montagues. They are new to the district. Just last summer. Although Col. Audley is newer but not really. He came from London last October, but Ridings is his family home. He just hasn't lived here in a long time, not in the entire time that Papa has been vicar."

Toby seized her hand. "You're shivering. We should head back." And he kept his grip as they came off the height.

By the time they reached the tree-lined lane, Melly no longer shivered. The trees offered a tempting distraction. He dragged her beneath the cover of an overhanging oak and pressed her against the bark.

"Oh my," she said and placed her hands on his shoulders. "Am I about to be ravished?"

"Not quite."

"I'm disappointed."

He grinned. "I do want to kiss you."

"Please do." She offered her mouth for one of the chaste kisses he'd given her in London.

Toby didn't want chaste. He wanted reckless. He wanted abandoned. He wanted her to know how deeply she affected him.

But if he took her back as rumpled as he wanted to make her, her father would toss him out on his ear.

So he gave her a chaste kiss. And then another one a little past chaste. Her fingers curled around his nape and threaded into his hair. "Open your mouth," he asked, and when she complied, he let her taste his desire. She moaned, and he nearly lost his head. He wanted to possess her. She wasn't his, just almost his, and it wasn't enough.

They were both breathing heavily when he drew back. Her lips were reddened, and when she touched her tongue to them, he nearly went back for more kisses.

"We shan't need the Scottish Highlands," she said. He'd lost the thread, and it took him a moment to pick up where the words had first been said.

His hands tightened on her waist. He hated the heavy coat that protected her from the cold. "If you want Scotland—."

Her hands tightened on him. "I want you, not Scotland." Then she gave a shaky laugh. "Or Scotland enough for Gretna Green."

"Miss Ratcliffe, are you proposing?"

"You have been most remiss, Toby. I thought you would say the words on the heights, but no, you talked about houses. And mountains."

"Your father—."

"Hang my father."

He laughed. "Your father, Miss Ratcliffe, will marry us from the Little Houghton Church. He will announce the banns beginning this Sunday."

"Have you talked with him already? Matthew and Miranda said you talked of your drive from London and the state of the roads."

"Eavesdropping, were they?"

"Like good little spies."

He gave her a sharp look, but her eyes remained guileless of additional intent. "I have something for you, burning a hole in my pocket."

"Toby," she gasped. "I was teasing."

"You don't want to be married to me?"

"I do." Her fingers threaded into his hair. "Oh, I do, Toby, but— have you spoken to my father yet?"

"He knows the reason I'm here. He didn't toss me out on my ear. He sent us off together. I'll ask his permission tonight, but I want my ring on your finger from this moment." Retaining his left-hand grip on her, he began digging under his greatcoat for his vest pocket.

When he drug it out, she started at it then withdrew her hands. "No. I mean not yet. My hair's a mess. I have on this old greatcoat. I wanted to be in silks and with candlelight."

"We can wait."

"Don't you dare."

He laughed and opened the little box. The fading sunlight sparkled in the white gemstones surrounding the central sapphire. "It's a family ring. Worn by several Kennit brides."

"I hope I am worthy of it." She sounded a little breathless.

He pushed the box back into a pocket then took her hand. "Melinda Ratcliffe, Melly, you have captured my heart with your joy, with your warmth, with your mind. Since that night, far back in November, when we met across a table of cards, I have wanted to claim you for my own. Before I met you, I had no purpose. You have given me a purpose. I want to create a home with you, a family of our own, and I want to grow old with you. Will you marry me?"

She extended a tremulous hand. "Yes, please, Toby. I feel the same. I want the same. I should have thought of what to say. Oh, Toby."

"Yes is enough." He slipped the ring on her finger.

She stared at the shining ring then flung her arms around him. She kissed his neck, his chin, then finally his mouth, opening hers as soon as his tongue touched her lips.

When he drew back this time, she followed him with little kisses until he had to set her firmly back. "We have to get back."

"I like living in alt," she pouted.

He laughed at that. Taking her newly ringed hand, he led her back onto the lane and toward the vicarage. "Do you still miss the silks and candlelight?"

"Not at all. But the banns had better be spoken starting this Sunday."

Melly sounded quite determined. That pleased Toby down to his toes.

Chapter 4 ~ Tuesday, 3 March 1812

Little Houghton

Eugenie tucked her change into her purse as she came down the steps from the shop. She slipped her purse into her embroidered reticule. Only then did she look up and nearly stumbled on the brick pavers.

A man walked along the other side of the street. She knew that sharp-nosed profile. She remembered how that hair fell forward over his high brow. She knew that long and lean stride.

Keiran Delaney. Or Jean Louis Jettere, depending on which persona he needed to assume.

He passed on, giving her only his back. He hadn't paused at all. He hadn't seen her.

But it was Delaney. Changed very little in the past eight years. When they'd met, Louis had told her Delaney was in his early twenties. He must be thirty now. A man. And the man across the street had no signs of youth. He looked hardened.

Just as she had hardened.

He hadn't seen her. He'd walked on without pause.

Keiran Delaney would never have acknowledged seeing an old associate. He wouldn't make that mistake.

Eugenie realized she was still standing, struck still by the past of Paris walking the street, as ominous as a bell tolling. She forced herself to continue on her way, but she was shaking.

She regained her composure by the time she reached the vicarage. The maid admitted her but let Eugenie find her own way to the upstairs room set aside for Miranda's art lessons. This morning she had hoped to see Melly and her mother. Now she hoped that she saw neither woman. Removing her hat before a mirror, she saw herself pale, too pale. Her hands still had a slight tremor.

She pinched her cheeks, rubbed her lips together. When the door opened, she turned to greet her pupil.

Miranda came in. "Mrs. DesChamps, look what I drew for today."

She took the foolscap from the girl. The paper shook. She had to set it on the table. With effort, she bent her attention to the drawing of the knot garden. "Mirry, this is well done. I like this view. Did you do it from this floor or the one above?"

"From the old nursery. Can you tell the different plants?"

"I can. You did very well with the shapes." She named each in turn, taking her time, then rested a nail on a little shape on the path. "What is this? A little rabbit?"

"He's not quite right."

"He will be run out of your mama's garden, I think. But it is clearly a rabbit." She looked up and met anxious eyes. "This is very good, Mirry. You did well with this lesson. And you stretched your limits. That is always good. Did you decide to add the rabbit, or did you see him?"

"I saw him."

"He will definitely be run out of your mama's garden." She slipped onto a chair and indicated that the girl should take the other. "Now, tell me where you struggled." As they talked, Eugenie's nerves calmed from the missed encounter outside the shop.

Miranda fetched her papers. She paid close attention as Eugenie mapped out the next lesson, developing the various shapes needed to draw a larger rabbit. She showed the girl how to use shading to develop the weight of the creature. She showed her a cat with long whiskers. Mirry's chuckle was her reward.

As she drew a puppy with big paws and floppy ears, Melly came in. She took the window seat while Eugenie showed Mirry how to shape a horse with long legs and swishing tail. Then she aimed the pencil at the girl. "You try."

"I can't—."

"You can. Look what you did without instruction. Practice the shapes before you put them together. Mistakes are fine. We are practicing, aren't we?"

The girl nodded. Eugenie rose from her seat and joined Melly.

"I like how you support her," Melly whispered. "Our previous governess did not tolerate mistakes."

"I remember your telling me that." She compressed her lips then said, "I saw a stranger in the village. He was walking toward the inn. Do you know of him?"

"Tall, dark hair, sharp features? That is my Tobias Kennit."

"Yours?"

"Yes," she said with a decided tone.

"This is the man you met in London? The one that Josette Sourantine introduced to you? The gamester." She remembered how Delaney had flirted scandalously in Paris. She remembered how he had strung along several ladies, both as Keiran Delaney and as Lieutenant Jettere.

"He is certainly taking a gamble on me," and she extended her left hand.

Eugenie saw the flashing ring. "Melly, he proposed?"

"And I accepted."

She admired the ring. When she finished with her compliments, she asked, "When will you marry?"

"The first Sunday in April. Papa approves."

"That is soon. Very soon." Her placid little life was ending. Her heart was breaking. "You have known him so little time."

"All those weeks in London while Great-Aunt Cordelia was ill. He escorted me to Josette's wedding. And we have corresponded for weeks."

Miranda interrupted her drawing. "Mr. Kennit came all the way to Little Houghton to court Melly. He arrived yesterday. I saw them kissing."

"You didn't," Melly said, but her color was high.

"I did. You were beneath the twisted oak in the lane. I didn't tell Mama, though. What's kissing like?"

As Melly struggled to explain, Eugenie grieved that her safe little world had tossed itself topsy-turvy, and she hadn't even realized it. She waited until Melly finished her vastly incomplete explanation, then asked, "A wedding in April. Will you be ready?"

"I may request your skills in embroidery, but I think we shall be. Mama is worrying about the breakfast after, but everything will be ready. She will not countenance anything else."

Knowing Mrs. Ratcliffe, Eugenie could only nod as Melly continued to describe the plans for the wedding and the reception, settled just that morning.

Tobias Kennit. Keiran Delaney. Kennit.

And she recalled how twice Sir Roger Nazenby had slipped. He shouldn't have said *Ken-* to her. Did he know Kennit had come to Little Houghton? Did he even remember that she had settled into a little cottage here? Did he care that two former spies were thrown together once more?

Did Kennit still work for the English spycatcher?

Melly had seized a sheet of Mirry's foolscap to draw a simple design of flowers and vines. "Can you finish that in a fortnight? We can piece it in as the bodice. Won't it look pretty? All pinks and violets and greens."

"A touch of blue, a touch of yellow, a touch of red. Yes, I can finish this in two weeks. You are serious? You are not—how do you say?—pulling my leg?"

"Very serious."

"I keep telling her *marry in haste, repent at leisure*."

"Mirry! I told you not to read *The Olde Batchelor*. Father will *not* be pleased."

Mirry was chastened not at all. "I did read it. I thought there were some funny parts. I didn't get most of it, though."

"And so you shouldn't. If Papa knew—."

"He doesn't. And you won't tell him. Or I will tell him what you and Mr. Kennit were doing at the twisted oak."

"Engaged couples are supposed to kiss," Melly countered, but her face flamed.

"Come," Eugenie said. "You are supposed to be concentrating on cats and horses. What have you drawn for me?" She seated herself at the table to look over the girl's work.

All the while wondering what she would say to Tobias Kennit when she met him.

. ~ . ~ . ~ .

London

Poulaine took a chair without waiting for Saultsein to offer it. "Do you have the man I need?"

"You gave me little time to work," the man complained.

The Frenchman merely stared at Saultsein. He'd been surprised when he learned Jacques Saultsein, known in London as Jack Salsby, still lived in his *pied à terre* on Charges Street. Then, remembering the man's reputation in Marseilles, he hadn't been surprised. Thierry and LeBrun had never wanted to deal with Saultsein. He'd never tried to overcome his street beginnings, and he'd honed his street-garnered skills in the years he'd worked as a spy.

Thierry and LeBrun had turned on their compatriots, but they had not dared to mention Saultsein to the English. He would have found a way to kill them, even as well guarded as they were in the English prison. LeBrun, facing execution, would prefer the civilized way that the English killed over Saultsein's way. The French spymaster took his time.

Two weeks ago Poulaine had visited the old haunts. He uttered the name 'Salsby' and his own hotel to only two men. That very night he'd found one of those men waiting when he left a nearby brothel.

Saultsein had needed no credentials. He remembered Poulaine. They had worked the same side of the spy game, cutting off loose threads and closing off escape routes. Both had gradually shifted to additional work.

Poulaine parleyed with his equal, but he wanted answers, and he wasn't willing to bargain. His purpose in England had expanded. His superiors demanded that he return with the cryptographer. He wanted Madame de la Croix to fulfill his personal vendetta.

"I have little time to waste. Do you have a man who can get the information I need from the English department?"

Saultsein allowed a little lift of his upper lip. "I do. He should arrive momentarily."

"Who is this man?."

He swirled the wine in the cut-glass goblet then sipped it appreciatively. "The English think he's one of the Hapsburg Germans. They hired him immediately when they realized he could translate everything from Russian to a Hungarian dialect. He has a special talent for languages."

"Trustworthy?"

"Completely. He has seen my work. He pissed himself."

Poulaine grinned at that, and Saultsein allowed himself another lift of his lip.

A tap on the door, then it opened. The butler bowed. "Sir, Mr. Stellensgard has arrived."

"Yes, he is expected. Send him in."

The butler stepped back to admit Stellensgard. Poulaine had a brief view of the other man in the hall, tall and broad, a pugilist by the look of his smashed face. He stood opposite the door, stationed there since the French spymaster's arrival. The butler was slim and sharp-featured. Poulaine trusted neither of them. In his own home, the big man would be the muscle while the butler would be the poisoner.

Stellensgard was neither muscle nor sly poisoner, and Poulaine didn't like the man on sight. He affected a forward comb of his thinning hair. Starched shirtpoints grazed his sunken cheeks, and his lurid waistcoat of puce and green hurt the Frenchman's eyes. His manners matched those of a fop.

The informant was not offered a seat. His quick look at the remaining chairs drawn around the fire betrayed that he had cozed with Saultsein on previous visits. But he didn't ask for a seat, and he did not seem surprised when Saultsein did not introduce Poulaine. He folded his hands before him and waited.

The Frenchman hid his distaste of the fop and concentrated on his purpose in coming to London. Very carefully he detailed the cryptographer's exploits.

Stellensgard was nodding before he was complete, but he waited until Poulaine finished his list. "Yes, yes, I know this man. We are in awe of his work. But he's not in our office. He never comes in. His contact is a man in White Hall who passes his work on to my chief, Mr. Pharis. Master A, we call him."

The man described a dead end, but no street was truly a dead end. Doors and windows offered other accesses. Even walls could be climbed. "You know this man's office?"

"Same as ours."

"You said he was not in your office."

"What I said was that he never comes in. He hands it off to the man in White Hall. That man sends it to Mr. Pharis, who merely approves his work and sends it to the higher-ups. But Master A is part of our division."

"You have never met him."

"He never comes—."

"I heard. Who first called him Master A?"

"I don't know. I'll ask, not too closely, just in passing. You get a lot of information that way. You get more over pints and even more when they're gambling."

Poulaine cast his eyes skyward as a man half his age tried to tell him how to spy. "Do you know anything about the man in White Hall who is Master A's contact?"

"I've never seen him."

"I asked if you knew anything about him."

"I've heard—just heard—that he is a great spycatcher. The execution in January of that French spy, they were caused by this man. Not many know about that execution."

Saultsein shifted in his upholstered chair before he entered the conversation. "I may know somewhat of this man in White Hall. We will talk of him later. For now, let us concentrate on this Master A."

"Indeed," Poulaine agreed. "Your information is helpful to me, and I appreciate it." He waited until Stellensgard had preened before he added, "Mr. Salsby says that you deal in a variety of documents. You are allowed to go into records storage? Good. I have an additional task for you. I wish you to find any information that you can about a Eugenie de la Croix. A French agent in Paris. She worked for the English from '01 to '06, when we lost track of her in Belgium. Her name may be associated with a Louis Langlais de la Croix, to whom she was married."

"Eugenie de la Croix. I'll do my best."

"Excellent. I expect results quickly."

The fop glanced at Saultsein. "I've been working on Master A for some time, Mr. Salsby. I thought information about him would want to be known. I think I am close to identifying him. Once I have that, I can find his location as well. I need to confirm a few details."

"Bring me that information, same price as before."

"With a bonus if you bring it within a couple of days," Poulaine offered.

Stellensgard looked at him, looked at Saultsein for confirmation. Then he nodded. "I will bend all my efforts to that."

"And to Madame de la Croix."

"Of course."

"That's all, Stellensgard."

"Yes, sir." He bowed to his master, hesitated then bowed as well to Poulaine. The door opened at his approach. He didn't seem unnerved by the burly guard, just made certain not to brush to closely to the man. His heels clacked as he walked away.

"And who is this Eugenie de la Croix?"

Poulaine narrowed his eyes. Round-bellied Saultsein was quick on the mark. He would ferret out most of the information on his own, but Poulaine might win a little bit more of his trust if he gave him the information. In his native language he said, "A French traitor. She stole information and gave it to the English. She escaped my net in `04."

"Speak English. What Mac hears in English, he ignores. French sharpens his ears."

"He speaks French?"

"He doesn't. But he works for Jack Salsby, not anyone else. Do you understand?" At Poulaine's nod, he picked up his wine. He also picked up on a seeming discrepancy. "You told Stellensgard that you lost track of this de la Croix woman in `06."

"I tracked her to Brussels. I lost all trace of her there. Now I find she is in London." He toasted the air and the sheer chance that had enabled him to find her. "I believe I have found a clue to her whereabouts."

"A clue in London? Have you found the proverbial needle?"

"The Langlais residence had several landscapes. Paris scenes, with several near their St. Germain residence. The artist had a special touch. He was especially gifted in his depictions of radiant light. I have a few of the paintings from that residence. I confiscated them when the de la Croix woman fled Paris. I did not realize until just recently that she must have fled with the artist who painted them."

"Have you thought that she is this artist?"

"I have not thought that. She is no more than a flirt, a *putain* that Langlais used." Eugenie had lifted her hand to very little.

But she had chattered all the way from Chartres to Paris as if she had not seen him murder Foucault.

Is she the artist? Poulaine thought again of the landscape in his lodgings. E. DesChamps. In all the people who had visited the Langlais hotel, none were artists of that caliber. Had she painted those Paris scenes? Had she painted the scene of a murder that haunted her?

Eugenie DesChamps.

Annette had never revealed her last name. His visit to Saumer had not revealed her family. Poulaine had not been interested in locating her relatives. A mistake he now recognized.

No, that was a leap. Eugenie de la Croix had had few talents. A gift with paintbrush and oils was not one of them. Somehow, she had either traveled with the artist or re-connected with him. She had described the scene to him. Find the artist. She would be only a few steps beyond.

"*Ce n'est pas possible*," he told Saultsein.

"And the connection to London?" Saultsein's voice did not sound interested, but his eyelids flickered before he asked the question.

Poulaine smiled behind his wineglass and gave part of the answer. "A simple English landscape that the gallery owner told me was of the Yorkshire moors.

"I assume the artist had a gift with radiant light."

"And signed the canvas E. DesChamps."

"I admit to a curiosity to see this painting—and its artist. And eventually, your target."

"You may see her only if you go to Paris. I intend to find her, take her back, and escort her myself to her execution. Now, tell me what you know of this spycatcher, the one who is the contact for Master A."

"The execution in January was LeBrun. You know that. The man who ordered the execution was Sir Roger Nazenby."

Poulaine reared back. "Nazenby? Nazenby? I know this name. I met a man named Nazenby many years ago in Paris. He was with the diplomats seeking an exchange of prisoners. He kept to the background. He was not important at that time. Is this the same man?"

"The man that I know of is your English counterpart."

"I have no counterpart. I am unique."

Saultsein lifted his lip again. "You want his location?"

"I am here for the cryptographer. I want also the French traitor Madame de la Croix. I want her associates in Paris: Keiran Delaney and Jean Louis Jettere. This Nazenby, he does his job. We do not want him removed. We can watch him. We can learn more that way. He might lead us to Delaney and Jettere."

"That's true. I will pull back my hounds then."

"You already have them in place?"

"I try to anticipate needs." Saultsein stood, an indication that he given as much time to this meeting as he intended. "Anticipating keeps me in business and keeps me safe. My men will watch, nothing else, not until it is necessary."

Poulaine did not comment. Results earned his respect, not bragging. He needed to move forward. He had another meeting, a man who might give him a line on Keiran Delaney. Through Delaney, he had another route to find Eugenie de la Croix. He would not leave England without her.

.~.~.~.

Reilly did not serve him wine. His chairs were hard wood, and the fire smoked more than it threw out heat.

He admitted Poulaine with a repressed snarl and turned his back on the Frenchman as he stomped back to his chair. He picked up his stout and drank deeply while Poulaine seated himself on the other side of the fire.

"Long time," Reilly said and pushed a stout in Poulaine's direction.

As he drank, he looked around the shabby room and noted the man's stretched sweater over heavy drill. In Paris, Reilly had dressed to match other Irish ex-pats. He wondered what game the man was running. "I may have a job for you."

His grin flashed whitely in the dim room. "If it fits with the game I'm running, sure. Never expected to see you surface in London, Poulaine."

"These are not the environs you were accustomed to in Paris."

Reilly shrugged and drank again. "What can I do for you?"

"I understand you are working with your compatriots to disrupt as many government operations as you can."

The frown was quick, followed by another wide grin. "Now where did you hear that information? Same place as got you my lodgings?"

"Saultsein keeps watch."

"He would. I got my plans. You want in?"

"I came to offer a distraction you may find welcome. If you still want to find Keiran Delaney."

Reilly swore. "I don't want to find him. I want to cut his throat. Can you give me that?"

"Very likely."

"I'd drop plans to shoot the Regent himself if I could get hands on Delaney. What you got?"

"Nothing yet. A small piece of a puzzle, but I believe it is the crucial piece. I want to enlist your aid if the piece comes into my hand as I expect it to do so."

The Irishman's pause had nothing to do with hesitation. "For this, Poulaine, I'm your man. Delaney got six of my men killed. He set us back a decade, more than that. You tell me when and where, and I'll bring the knife."

"Excellent."

They shook hands, each of them contemplating deaths they had long anticipated.

Chapter 5 ~ Wednesday, 4 March 1812

Little Houghton

Eugenie woke in a foul mood. She ate her breakfast in a distracted manner, then she went straight to her studio. Yesterday's work rested on the easel. She replaced it with a blank canvas. Without even sketching the scene, she began laying oil onto the canvas.

The maid brought her tea and stirred up the fire. Eugenie didn't notice.

The girl cleared her throat. "Mrs. DesChamps, you said we might have a visitor today."

"*Qu'est que c'est*? Ah, Clarrie, just our regular tea."

"You mentioned tartlets, ma'am. Sweet and savory, you said."

She stared at the golden field and the blue, blue sky. "You know what to do, Clarrie."

"Yes, ma'am, but——."

Her mistress didn't look around. The maid sighed and retreated.

When next Eugenie looked up, she realized she had filled yet another canvas with the scene that haunted her. She burned most of those canvasses; Clarrie must think her deranged. With much misgiving she had sent the last one to London. Her agent had pressed for a larger landscape; she had had nothing else to send him. And now she had created another.

At least that canvas hadn't depicted the murder. If she let this one dry, she would have to burn it as well. Another waste of good canvas and oils.

Louis had asked her to travel to Chartres with Didier Poulaine. She had protested: *I do not trust this man. I do not like this man.* Louis had merely said, *You must do it. I cannot. He will not offer offense to you my wife.*

No, he had offered her no offense. He had suggested that she tour the Cathedral while he conducted his business. She had followed him instead. She had followed—and watched him kill a man. The hardest hours of her life had been to climb back into the closed carriage with a man she knew to be a murderer and chat carelessly about little nothings.

Louis had soothed her hysterics when she returned to their Paris *appartement*. She had watched murder. Her soul felt stained because she had done nothing to help the man or to report the criminal. She did not even know the man's name. Louis knew it, she was certain, but he didn't share it with her. She did not even know the reason for the man's death. And the next evening she had to entertain Poulaine and other guests and never let slip what she'd seen.

Eugenie scraped the oils off the canvas. Then she scrubbed a rag over the oil stains.

The red blotch of the murder glared at her. She slapped white over it and considered the shoreline at Staithes.

The London agent might let her replace that canvas with a new one. People liked the shoreline. They liked the moors. Surely he would return that canvas if she asked him to do so? She would send him two for that one.

"Mrs. DesChamps?"

She didn't look up from her sketch blocking out the masses of the cliff and the ocean and the shoreline. Already she could see the sun glinting on the rock face, ochre and umber and sienna above the golden shoreline, complemented by the blue sky. "Yes, Clarrie?"

"Col. Audley will arrive at three o'clock, ma'am."

"Yes?"

"It's two o'clock, ma'am. You ignored your luncheon."

She glanced around and saw the untouched tray on her desk. "Oh, my!" Hastily, she tossed her pencil onto her desk and jerked at her painting smock. Clarrie came forward to untie it for her. "I didn't realize so much time had passed."

"You were at the scene again, the one you told me you couldn't set right. Oh, ma'am, your hands."

She stared at the paint stains. A splotch of red marred her left-side thumb. Strange, that the color was there when she painted with her right hand. Red on the sinister side. She shuddered with premonition.

"I laid out your primrose dress, ma'am."

"The tea, Clarrie?"

"The tartlets will go in next, ma'am. Never you worry about that. I followed the receipt like you showed me last time. I do think I did a fine job with the pastry."

"I shouldn't have shown you how to make pastry. The next thing I know, someone will be stealing you away from me."

"I wouldn't leave you, ma'am."

"If they offered you more money, of course you should leave me, Clarrie."

She dashed upstairs to change. Most of the paint scrubbed off her hands, all but the brightest and darkest of colors. She was slipping into the gown when Clarrie appeared to lace her up. Then the maid went back downstairs to keep an eye on the tartlets. Eugenie brushed her hair out. She was reaching for the pins when the doorbell jangled.

She swept her hair back with the first ribbon that came to hand then considered gloves. But Col. Audley knew she painted. He was here to talk about buying a painting from her. She slipped into light shoes and hurried out of her chamber.

Clarrie was admitting the colonel. Handing off his coat to the maid, he looked up then stood arrested as she came down the steps. She could not have wanted a better effect with her entrance.

"Col. Audley." She reached the slate floor that Clarrie must have scrubbed this morning and offered her hand.

He reached for it, realized he still held his gloves, transferred them to his other hand, then bent over her offered hand. The paint splotches didn't affect him. He didn't kiss her hand, but for a courtier's gesture, he performed it very well.

Then he handed off his gloves and hat to the maid. Clarrie risked a roll of her eyes at her mistress before she disappeared into the back of the house.

Asking about his drive from his house seemed foolish. "Would you like to see my studio?"

"And catch a glimpse of the artist's work? Yes."

He glanced at the canvas on which she had sketched the Staithes shoreline then continued on to the half-finished canvas of the moors that she had discarded this morning. Eugenie was relieved that she had scrubbed away the murder painting.

Audley studied the moors landscape. He didn't lift it from the floor, but he stood before it for some time. "I like this," he finally said, "but it is not what I want. It's not as good as *Un Reve de Paix.* You are trying for a snowy landscape?"

She came closer. "It will sell," she defended.

"Ah, French practicality."

"I am French."

He turned his head, and she earned a bit of the smile that had first attracted her last fall. He gestured to the blocked canvas on her easel, the sketch forcing the lines of the wiped-out oils into new shapes. "But you abandoned it, for cliffs beside the sea. That's a technique that I haven't seen, back-painting the canvas."

She wasn't about to tell him that she had abandoned the snowy moors for a murder scene that haunted her. "That, too, will sell."

"More quickly, I would judge, than snows in Yorkshire. Not enough drama."

She bent her stained left thumb inside her palm. "No, not enough drama," she agreed. "I need just a little more, but not too much."

Clarrie interrupted them with words of the tea.

The colonel was properly appreciative of the tartlets, but he had scarcely demolished a half-dozen before he was trying to convince her to drive back to Ridings with him. "I want you to see the scene. Today is the perfect day. We have just enough clouds, just enough wind, to inspire you. It is not a scene of high drama. It reminds me of God and man." He looked abashed at that statement, but he didn't retract it. "Should you see it today, you will know I am right. Give me a half-hour of your time, no more."

"And a quarter-hour to drive there and another quarter-hour back, and the day is over, Col. Audley."

"I thought we were to be Charles and Eugenie. Are you relegating me back to distant status?"

She didn't know how to answer. She had not wanted to seem too friendly or too eager for his company. Instead, she deflected. "I cannot go with you to your home. It is already half-past three."

"Have you another commission that's pressing? Or just a landscape to provide to the London gallery owner?"

She had no good answer to that. The only image haunting her was the one of golden fields in Chartres, with a red smear that marred the glory of the day.

Clarrie came in with another pot of tea, and Eugenie found herself asking the maid to collect her greatcoat and gloves. "The colonel and I are going for a drive."

The maid stared then said, "Yes, ma'am." But when she helped Eugenie into her greatcoat, she whispered, "Ma'am, is this wise? He is not well known to you."

"He is commissioning a landscape, Clarrie. And the money will be helpful. The general has not mentioned when he will pay me for his wife's portrait."

"There are only servants at his house, ma'am."

She faced the maid. Her bravery was already faltering. "Is he not a man to be trusted? Are there rumors about him?"

"Nothing like that. But your reputation—."

The answer somehow bolstered her decision to go his home. "I think my reputation can withstand a half-hour in his house."

When she put her hand into Audley's so he could assist her into the pony cart, she gave him a narrow-eyed look. He started in surprise, then he looked at her maid, still standing in the open doorway.

"Have you been warned about me?"

"According to Clarrie, there are no rumors about you. Should I be warned?"

"Of course not." He settled beside her and flicked the rug over her knees to keep her warm. Then he gathered up the reins and chucked to the horse. The cart started up. "It would be disappointing to have rumors with no reality to back them up. I live a very boring life, Eugenie."

So, he was determined to remain on first-name basis. "I am glad to hear that," and she dared herself to add "Charles. I do not seek drama."

"Only in your paintings."

"Of course. The people who purchase my landscapes, that is what they want. The blowing wind, the driving snow, the turbulent heavens, a lone person—."

"Or a lone tree."

"Yes, a lone person or tree against the elements. We see such a situation, representing a conflict of some sort, and we think *I will stand against this storm*."

The cart bounced over a rut, throwing her against him. She righted herself and put a hand on the rim to steady herself.

"Was it a storm that drove you from France?"

"Several storms. Look, see that bird. It looks like a robin. Harbinger of spring."

They drove in silence for some minutes. The chimneys of Ridings came into view before he said, "I can understand your reluctance to discuss anything in your past. I am not probing for information."

"A lie," she said quickly. "You disappoint me, Col. Audley. I did not think I would hear a lie from you, not today."

"My apologies. I would like to know your past, but only what you are willing to share." He took a deep breath then added, "I would like to know many things about you."

She looked away from the tall chimneys above the cluster of trees and gaped at him. Then she turned her head aside without comment.

"Have I embarrassed you?"

"You have left me not knowing what to say."

"I think I had better shut my mouth. That was, indeed, a robin."

He drove farther then turned off the main road onto the side road that would take them to his manor. The silence grew and grew until Eugenie was bursting with the need to speak.

"I do not talk of my past, you understand. My family is all gone, many years ago. I have no one left in France. My husband—he died over a decade ago."

"You were married very young."

"I had seventeen years." She remembered how lost she had felt.

She remembered how massive Paris had seemed. She remembered not knowing where to turn—and Louis Langlais, one of her father's contacts, had given her a direction. "He was kind to me. He was English. It was not wise for him to be in France, you understand. He pretended to be French."

"So you married a Frenchman only to discover he was English."

"*Non.* I knew he was English. *Mon pere*, he told me of this *Anglais*, a man he trusted, he said. Since the French authorities had arrested *mon pere*, I did not trust the French authorities."

"Your father was arrested?"

"He spoke against Bonaparte's government. He wished to return to the ideals of the Revolution: *liberte, egalite, fraternite.* Those are gone now."

"So you married your Englishmen, and when he died, you came to England."

How little I am actually telling him! "With a few detours in my journey, but yes."

The red-bricked stories of Ridings rose above them. He stopped the cart. A groom ran up to take the horse's head. A servant in dun-colored livery left the house. He dropped down the step then opened the carriage door and stood back. By then, Audley had circled around the horse and given her his hand. Eugenie stepped down then followed Audley into his home.

The manor was well tended. She had noticed the lawn, still brown but swept clean of debris. The hedges were clipped carefully to keep them off the drive while retaining their natural shape. The entrance hall had the same care: waxed wood and polished brass. The wall paneling would have darkened the hall, but well-placed lights kept it looking cheery.

Her coat and gloves were taken away. Audley was murmuring to the older servant, then he turned to her. "My study is this way. Are you ready to see it, or do you need to retire for a bit? I understand women wish to freshen themselves."

"I wish to see this scene that has you dragging me from my home on this windy day to show me the scene you wish painted." There, those words should give the servants something reasonable to chatter about instead of inventing gossip.

His mouth crooked, as if he understood the motive behind her words. "This way, Mdm. DesChamps."

The study echoed the entrance hall's dark paneling, relieved by volumes of books that she wanted to peruse. "Do you have any French authors?"

"Montaigne. Moliere. Montesquieu. Marivaux. Voltaire."

"Good. For a brief second, I thought you limited to authors whose names began with M."

He chuckled, which gladdened her heart. Some people did not understand her form of wit. "I have Moritz and Machiavelli and Marlowe if you are willing to branch about beyond the French." He reached two glass-paned doors at the end of the study and opened them, admitting a wind off the moors.

Eugenie did not exclaim at the cold air but came up behind him. When he stepped onto the bricked terrace, she followed. As she stopped beside him, she spared him a glance. He seemed taller here, which was foolishness, for a man could not grow inches between her house and his. At her little house he should have seemed much taller. Yet somehow, here at Ridings, looking at the wild moor behind the manor, Charles Audley appeared different.

She turned her gaze upon the moor and immediately saw the reason he wanted this view memorialized. "Ah, *oui*."

"You see it then, that wildness that tugs at my soul. A mystery that cannot be known. Like God himself."

"I see that." And she did. The upswelling of a land that could never be tamed. The very elements of the moor would prevent it from ever being tamed. "We are the cultivated fields of the tamed land, so ... mundane, and the moors are like God himself, the creator so—so—."

"So unfathomable."

"*Oui*," she breathed.

He turned and looked down at her. She didn't lift her gaze to him, but kept surveying the moors. "But not majestic. This is not a place of majesty. For that, we would need the Alps."

That tugged her gaze to him. "The Alps are majestic. But I prefer your English moors. When did you see the Alps, Charles?"

"Years ago. And you?"

"With my family when I was a girl. Before my older brother joined the Army." She grinned. "The French side of the Alps, obviously."

He laughed, which pleased her. "I saw the Italian side. I had gone to a monastery for information—well, that is a boring story," and he broke it off. "Will you do the landscape, Eugenie?"

"You want this specific scene?"

"The moor. Clouds rolling from the west. Perhaps blue skies on the east. Green fields."

"The moors in bloom would create an expanse of color."

"You know the colors of the heather. You won't need to wait until summer."

She looked back at the uplands. Clouds were rolling in from the west, just as he described, but here in March, she had discovered, the weather could be rain or sleet and snow. "I will do it. Supplies must be sent from York. I have a shop there that can supply what I need. I will write to them tomorrow. What size do you want the canvas to be?"

"Ah, that requires we go to a different room. Come with me."

He shut the glass-paned doors. The wind had sucked all warmth from the study. She glanced at the leaping fire; she had chilled as well, standing out on the terrace, but she followed him back to the entrance hall. He spoke to a footman as he passed. She didn't hear the words, but the man headed to the back of the house as she passed him.

Charles flung open a set of double doors and stepped back.

She entered a drawing room much larger than his study. A fire burned here as well, and the room had not lost any of its warmth to foolishness with exterior doors. Yet she understood that foolishness.

He led her to the fireplace, which she appreciated, then stood looking up at a life-size portrait. "That is an ancestor," she said. "This will be an expensive canvas, Charles." Quickly, she calculated the expense of canvas and stretcher as well as an appropriate frame, the price of oils and brushes, and the time it would take her. "I am afraid to tell you what it will cost."

"Cost is not the issue."

"Such words are reckless. I could inflate my price."

His head cocked to one side. "I trust you."

"That, too, is reckless. You know me very little. I could over-charge you."

"But how am I to know what an artist will charge? This landscape will be the centerpiece of this room. And much more pleasing to the eye than my Elizabethan ancestor with tights on his skinny legs."

She looked at the offending legs. "They are certainly skinny."

"Do you need a down-payment—for the canvas and oils?"

The general had not offered to pay her. She was not even certain that he would. Her agent had cautioned her against commissioned work for that very reason. "A percentage, to cover the canvas, certainly. That is a large expense for me. And I will want to come here a few times, with all my paraphernalia—to make small sections. I will not risk moving such a large canvas."

"You could work here. Leave the canvas up. There is room. Come, I will show you," and he headed back to the study.

Eugenie took another glance at the size of the Elizabethan ancestor that her landscape would replace. Then she followed him a second time. By the time she entered the study, Charles was at the far end of the room, pushing club chairs out of the way. Then he straightened and opened his arms wide before the glass-paned doors. "More than enough room."

She glanced at his desk, littered with papers and opened books, with spindled papers on the floor. "I would not wish to disturb you."

"That is nothing." He scooped up the spindled papers then chucked them into the fireplace. "Once I start working, I don't notice much. If my presence won't disturb *you*."

It was reassuring to hear that someone else became caught up in his work. "Clarrie has to stop me for tea and for meals. I missed lunch today because she was contending with the pastry for the tartlets. When I am painting, even when I am sketching, I can become lost in the scene. Perhaps that will remain the same if someone else is in the room, but—oils smell strongly, Charles. I grind and mix my own paints as I need them, which usually consumes the morning. And then the turpentine that I use to thin the paint and clean my brushes, that smells as well. And I may drop paint on the floor."

"We can lay down a heavy cloth. If the odor bothers me, I can choose another room to work in. Will you do it?"

Eugenie's eyes opened wide at how quickly he had dispensed with her objections. She glanced out the doors. "I do wish to paint this scene. I will sketch it first, and then perhaps I will do a small canvas, to test the colors."

"I feel like celebrating." He moved to the drinks tray. "What will you have? Sherry? Whisky? Cognac?"

She moved behind him. "You have the brandy?"

He looked over his shoulder. "I have French cognac, specially procured. Don't tell anyone. I fear I traded with a fence for smugglers to acquire it. A little shop in Ipswich."

She accepted the snifter and cupped it in both hands, for cognac should be warmed by body heat.

He saw the stains on her hands. "An accident with a canvas?"

She thought of the morning's work, scrapped and scrubbed away. "That is probably the best way to put it. A morning's work removed." She gave her Gallic shrug and pragmatic outlook. "I will paint again tomorrow, the cliffs at Staithes. And I will come Friday, if I may, for my first sketch and to get an idea of the colors I will need. I will use watercolors first. The colors are not so intense—nor the smell."

"Watercolors are not as intense as oils."

"I can check the blend of colors. Then I will write to the shop in York, to tell them what I need." She allowed herself to grin. "I begin to be excited by this landscape of yours."

He lifted his glass in a toast. "To better paintings then. To a painting worthy of my moors."

He clinked their glasses together. His gaze held hers as they drank the toast. Eugenie found that she could not look away. She didn't want to look away.

Chapter 6 ~ Friday, 6 March 1812

London

Poulaine entered the gallery. The shop assistant ducked into the back. A few seconds passed, then an older man emerged. His walk affected on little heels, he crossed to Poulaine.

"*Monsieur*, welcome to my gallery."

"You are *M'sieur* Rainsford?"

"Indeed, yes. My assistant tells me that you are interested in works by a particular artist."

"*Oui, le method.* The use of light with shadow—."

"Chiaroscuro."

Poulaine gave him a narrow-eyed look at being interrupted. "*Non*, not like the Rembrandt or da Vinci or Caravaggio. The way a beam of light comes through the clouds, yes? *Peut-etre votre assistant*, he did not comprehend so well."

"Of course. You have a particular type of scene in mind, not the technique used."

"The *Wild Moor*, you have this painting still?"

"Of course. My assistant said you expressed an interest in it." He guided him around a free-standing panel where the painting hung on the back side. "You wish to purchase it?"

"It is possible."

"We can deliver it to your lodgings—."

"I have a foible. That is the word, I think," Poulaine said, starting his lie. "I wish to see the place of the painting. I buy where I have been. You understand this? The other painting that I purchased, that is of a village I myself have visited. It is near the great cathedral of Chartres. The light, it is much as it is in the painting. I would not wish to purchase a painting of a place I have not known. Would you tell me the place this painting depicts?"

The gallery owner frowned. "I do not know the exact location, just that it is a depiction of the Yorkshire moors. The hinterlands compared to London." He gave a delicate shudder. "I dislike rural areas."

"The artist, he travels far afield for his locations?"

"No. Actually, I do not think she—he travels very far at all. In the letter accompanying the painting, the artist said this location was very close to home."

"Ah." Poulaine hid his excitement at the man's slip of tongue. The artist was a female. Since Saultsein's suggestions, he was beginning to believe the artist was Eugenie de la Croix herself. "Where is this house?"

The gallery owner hesitated. "The artist is very private."

"I do not seek the artist. I seek only the location. I can travel there this summer. Certain business will keep me in London until June."

"June would be the time to visit the moors. I understand snow can fall well into April."

"I am not one for the snow." He exaggerated his shudder. "Will you tell to me the name of the village of this location?"

The man hesitated again.

"I will take the painting with me when I visit these moors. To find the exact location. Then, when I see it above my fireplace, I am able to say, Here I have visited. A foible, yes?"

"I believe the correct word is eccentricity. I regret to inform you that the artist does not care for visitors."

"I do not wish to visit the artist, only the location."

"Nevertheless, I would break a trust if I gave you that location without permission. I can write to the artist and ask the specific location for this painting, if you wish it."

"I do so wish. How long before you receive a reply?"

"A fortnight, at least."

Too long. Poulaine knew the man had the answer on the tip of his tongue. He was angry enough to cut that tongue out—but he controlled his rage. "Your assistant informed me that you do not hold paintings for any time."

"A policy the previous owner of the gallery instituted which I maintain."

"*D'accord.* I will take this painting with me today, as a trust that you will provide the location after this fortnight."

"I may not receive permission—."

"We shall see, *oui*? *Maintenante*, I will pay now. My carriage is outside. See you, I brought it expecting to purchase. I have great faith in you, *M'sieur.*"

.~.~.~.

Little Houghton

Charles sneaked another look at Eugenie as she washed out a brush then frowned at the thick foolscap penned to her portable easel. When she left the brush in the waterpot and stepped back, he didn't pretend to ignore that.

"Problems?" for the foolscap had only a few strokes of color washed across it. Pink, purple and brown, with blue and slate in the sky.

"The colors are wrong. They are not—they do not reflect this place, this—they do not reflect you."

"The painting has to reflect me?"

She looked over her shoulder. "I seek a tantalizing image of you. Had I painted a landscape and you chose it, that would be a different matter. I think, however, that I must paint my view of you."

"Am I so difficult to capture?" Turning the cipher disk upside down, he stood up and crossed to her.

"You are not pink and purple like the heather, Charles."

He chuckled. "Watercolors and oils—."

"I think the problem may be the season. Which season do you want?"

"Which do you want to paint?"

She huffed. "I do not expect you care if the painting matches the furnishings."

"I would hope it doesn't." Eugenie rewarded him with a smile, so Charles ventured further. He bumped his shoulder against hers. "The heather in bloom?"

"Blue sky above?"

"I thought we were going for a storm."

"Breaking or gathering?"

He tilted his head and offered a grin. "Is there a difference?"

Her smile increased. "Only in our perspective."

"Grays," he countered, "and browns. The moors this winter. The rocks dominant."

She turned her head and studied him. "Slate clouds gathering across a blue, blue sky, the subtle variations of the moor below. Yes, this I see."

That didn't sound good. "You think I'm colorless?"

"I think you are like granite, and no storm could move you. You set yourself a course and follow it, no matter what obstacle is thrown up."

He wasn't certain she was flattering him. "You are making me sound stubborn. And you're talking about Sunday."

"And this day, watching you work at your desk. You do not grumble, you do not sigh in frustration, you do not break your pencil. You work away, spindle the useless, and continue on."

"I didn't think you were watching."

"I think I watched you as much as you watched me."

Charles was thankful that he didn't blush like a schoolboy. "Your work habits intrigue me. I've never watched a master artist create from nothing. I have only ever seen the finished product."

"I have never seen a master cryptographer develop a new cipher. I have worked with ciphers—."

He gripped her upper arm. "How did you—no one is supposed to know. How did you know what I was doing?"

She stared at his hand. He released her. She gave a little lift of her shoulder. "I have worked with ciphers, decoding messages. I have never encoded a message, but I have watched someone do so. And I know how to use that Vigenere cipher disk on your desk."

"Not many people know that. Only those of us in the communications bureau and ... spies."

Eugenie shrugged. "I left France under a cloud, Charles. I cannot go back. I will leave you to guess the reason."

He took her arm again, more gently this time, and guided her over to the chairs before the hearth. After he pulled the bell rope, he took the chair across from hers. "I suppose that's one of those things not to be spoken aloud. Just as my work is."

"I will not tell anyone, Charles. I understand the importance of your work and the necessity for secrecy."

"I trust you, Eugenie."

Her lashes lowered. Her smile was soft and small, not like her usual open smile that welcomed all but never quite reached her eyes. When she lifted her lashes, he saw tears shining in her eyes.

"Eugenie?"

"No, Charles, do not be concerned. Your trust makes me happy. One day I will explain, I promise. Just—not now, please."

"As you wish." The opening door and advent of the tea tray prevented anything else.

When she returned to her cottage and he stood alone before the windows, watching dusk consume the moors, he was grateful for the tea tray's interruption. He was a logical man with excellent reasoning capabilities. He should not have been on the verge of telling anyone about his ciphering. And while he might trust Eugenie DesChamps, Sir Roger Nazenby would erupt like Mt. Etna if he discovered Charles had revealed his work to the Frenchwoman.

.~.~.~.

Monday, 9 March 1812 ~ London

The small hours were the best for his bloodwork.

The woman died quickly and quietly. The man continued his

snoring without a break.

With streetlamps giving him all the light he needed, Poulaine walked with long-practiced stealth around the foot of the bed. He stopped the gallery owner's snores with his gloved hand, blocking his mouth and nose.

The man jerked from sleep. He heaved and brought his hands up—then froze when the dagger pricked his throat.

"*Bon, tres bon,*" Poulaine said, not bothering to lower his voice. The woman was the only other occupant of this floor. "Come from the bed."

The man's wide eyes revealed his fear. Poulaine removed his hand and gripped the collar of his nightshirt. Those wide eyes swiveled to the woman.

"She will not wake. Not ever again." He smelled urine as the man lost his water. Poulaine let the dagger touch the throat again and towed on the nightshirt.

He never understood how men could expect death and not fight. Surely the gallery owner understood the end coming to him with the woman already dead? But the man obeyed the order to sit on the stool Poulaine had placed in a shaft of light, and he sat quiescent as his hands were tied behind him.

Poulaine straightened and walked around the man before stopping before him. "Now, is it that you know the reason that I visit you?"

He shook his head.

"Are you so dumb?"

"No, I don't—I told you that I would write the letter."

"And I expect that you have written it?"

"I—I posted it yesterday."

"Yesterday would be Sunday. We are in the small hours of Monday."

"On Saturday! I posted it Saturday!"

"Voice down," he cautioned. The man gulped and nodded. "I repeat that I have expended my patience for the answer, *M'sieur*. If you please, tell me the location of the artist DesChamps."

"I do not have permission—."

"I do not argue with you. I have my persuasion." He let the light flash on the dagger's long thin blade. The gallery owner's eyes widened. "I know you know the location. Did you not write the letter to the artist DesChamps? You will tell me now."

"It's—It's Little Houghton. In Yorkshire. You can find it on any postal map."

"*D'accord.* Now we go to a harder question. Yes, you can answer this as well. The artist's privacy means nothing, you understand. Is the artist a man or a woman?"

"I shouldn't—. A woman. She's a woman."

Poulaine felt a little unhappy that the man needed no persuasion. Perhaps that was best. The servants above stairs and the man's neighbors would not be wakened if he remained cooperative. "And one last question, the hardest of all: what is the name of this artist?"

The man hesitated. Poulaine leaned forward. "DesChamps," he said hastily. "DesChamps."

"So, she signs a name. Could she also have the name of Eugenie de la Croix?"

"De la Croix I don't know, but—but—her first name is Eugenie."

"Ah, see? That was not so difficult. Now, close your eyes and stick out your tongue." The man looked confused. "Is that difficult? No. Close your eyes," he coaxed gently. "Open your mouth. Put out your tongue."

He gripped the tongue and introduced the dagger.

The man's scream was garbled. It wouldn't carry far. He kicked, but Poulaine made short work of the job. When he left, the gallery owner lay on the floor. He stripped off his gloves and dropped them on the floor before he walked out of the house.

Chapter 7 ~ Wednesday, 11 March 1812

Little Houghton

Kennit, the letter began, *I have stumbled upon a new novel that I believe you would find interesting. Let me describe the plot.*

Toby stared at the folded quarto. He flipped it again to the side with the broken seal. When the desk clerk had handed the letter to him, Toby had repressed a groan when he saw Roger Nazenby's seal. His former employer had not anticipated a need to contact him when they'd met in London. That Nazenby contacted him now and took the risky method of pen to paper meant that circumstances had changed. The man risked much by sending this letter even with a simple substitution code.

Not too dire a situation, or Nazenby would have sent a man—someone like Michael Armitage—to warn Toby personally.

The wind gusted, pushing against his window. He glanced at the night-darkened panes then focused on the letter.

The novel opens with a murder by an assassin seeking another person, Nazenby wrote in his sprawling script. *That certainly claimed my attention. I will admit that I stayed up very late trying to decipher the mystery; however, I am still only in the midst of the novel. The witness to the murder claimed not to know the identity of the murderer. A murder-for-hire, he also claimed. He did let slip that the man was French, but he knew no more.*

An assassin, hired by the French. What murder had alerted Nazenby? Or was it no murder but an attempted assassination or a murder to come? What had his London agents learned? Toby forgot the whisky he had poured and drew his chair closer to the fire.

The novel has three main characters. The importance of one those characters is as yet unknown to me. Believe me, I was quite surprised at the confluence of the three characters. The French agent encountered our hero and his heroine many years ago in Paris. He followed them to London. I am on tenterhooks to discover where the author has secreted this man as well as the identity of his associates. The French agent apparently swore vengeance many years ago when the hero and the heroine eluded his snare. The witness did not know the reason, only that they are sought.

Kennit re-read the last two sentences. Many years ago in Paris he had worked as a spy under the names Keiran Delaney and Jean Louis Jettere. One of his contacts had been Eugenie de la Croix. She had died, arrested by the French and executed. And the French agent who would have sworn vengeance could only be Didier Poulaine.

On many, many occasions Toby had dealt with the man, and every occasion had left a vile taste in his mouth. In the early days of the Revolution, Poulaine had hunted aristocrats and ensured they traveled by tumbrel to the guillotine. As the Revolution transformed, his job had transformed. While others were cast out and even executed for their deeds in the early days of the new republic, he had wiggled into new positions, first as a spy reporting on his former masters to the members of the *Directoire*.

By '02, when Toby had first encountered him, Poulaine had been running a division of internal French agents seeking counterspies. He had still performed the occasional assassination of men deemed too dangerous to be placed on public trial or private tribunal. He had bragged about his work to the French captain Jettere, never knowing that he rubbed elbows with an English counterspy.

How had Poulaine made his way to London?

Toby got up and paced the room. After the Sourantine woman's death and the arrest of the two master spies Robert LeBrun and Claude Thierry, Toby had hoped that any network of French spies in England would be too damaged to continue any work. Yet Poulaine the assassin boldly walked London's streets.

Poulaine could not be in England for revenge alone. He might hope to find the English counter-spy who had duped him and his agents, but his Paris masters would not release him to pursue personal vengeance. No, he had planted his feet on British soil for another reason. The capture of the master British cryptographer.

That primary goal might help him achieve his secondary goal of revenge. Poulaine would not care about the destruction in his wake.

Toby returned to his chair. First, he sipped some whisky. The wind rattled against the glass panes. He turned his head toward the window, but he didn't see it. He didn't see the room he stood in. His mind cast back to his last day in Paris.

The gates of the Bastille stood before him. "Jettere," he'd informed the guards. He stood straight in his French uniform. Delaney's disguise had been discarded on his return to Paris. He'd half-expected Jettere's lodging to have been tossed, but Poulaine's agent had missed that step in their hurry to pursue Delaney and to arrest Eugenie de la Croix. "I have a letter from General de Laurent Gouvion St. Cyr to M'sieur Berthier."

The guards muttered among themselves.

He slapped his gloves across his palm as he waited. Poulaine had tracked him north of Paris. Toby hoped the man had continued on to Calais. He would have had no reason to guess that Toby had turned back and planned to toss his own life into a risky gamble.

When a few minutes had passed, he allowed himself a bit of temper. "The general demands an answer today. He awaits my return. He does not expect that he must wait for the end of time."

"M'sieur Berthier is meeting with members of the Tribunal," one of the guards ventured.

"He will speak with me, I assure you. Admit me."

They had fallen back and allowed him to enter. His one fear was that one of the men would escort him to Berthier's office, but they let him continue into the prison without an escort.

Louis Langley, masquerading as Louis Langlais de la Croix, had once required him to memorize a draughtsman's plan for the Bastille. He'd obeyed the man's request without ever expecting to use it. If cornered, he planned to fight rather than submit to arrest. Yet he found himself grateful for Langley's required memorization. He took the few turns needed to lead him to the cells of the condemned.

The guards on duty there were drunk and slovenly. He let a fastidious distaste show as he demanded to be taken "to the cell of the traitoress de la Croix."

One of the guards was too drunk to do more than blink at him.

The other had leaned back on his chair. "We will miss her. Won't we, Etienne?" He took another swig from his bottle.

Etienne had laughed and rubbed his groin. "Miss her a lot. Never quite got my fill."

Toby had burned with the need to kill the man, to kill all of them. "Where is she? She is to serve witness before General de Laurent Gouvion St. Cyr. She has information about his son."

The first guard guffawed. "His great general-ness will have to send to God for that information."

"Or hell. Me, I think the little traitoress will be in hell."

"The way she was in hell with us?" And all three laughed.

"Where is she?"

"Executed, not an hour since."

The floor tilted, but Toby maintained his persona. "The general will want more the word of stinking Bastille guards. I will have to see her body. You," he pointed to the third guard. "Take me there."

The gap-toothed man in the morgue had stared blankly then hobbled away, guiding them with a lantern. Toby prodded the guard to go before him, and they followed the man to a second room where *corpses lay sprawled against a wall.*

He'd spotted Eugenie in the lantern's flickering light, but he had to wait for the guard to find her body. They had stripped her of clothes, and her body was covered with bruises old and new. Her face was almost unrecognizable. The glaze in her dead eyes seemed to accuse him of coming too late.

He had throttled the cell guard as they climbed the stairs back to the cells. He had killed the other two with knives, coming up behind them and cutting their throats. Blood spurted over the floor and gushed from their wounds. He dropped the knives and his stained gloves beside their bodies. Unstained, he walked out of Bastille and never looked back.

Nazenby had let him walk away from spying. The spycatcher had already heard about Eugenie de la Croix's death. He probably had also heard about her days of imprisonment and Toby's murder of the guards.

Toby's soul had felt black for many months.

His mind still felt black.

He picked up Nazenby's letter. He should let Poulaine find him. A fight with the Frenchman might help cleanse the memory.

Nazenby wrote: *When I closed the book last night, the hero had decided not to warn his friend about the French agent but to watch for strangers coming into his village.*

I find it an excellent book, and I am anxious to finish it. I advise you to find a copy and read closely, or you will miss many of the clues.

Nazenby continued for a half-page more, describing a walk beside the Thames and his dinner with the dowager Countess Eaton and her family at Eaton House.

Toby stared at Nazenby's scrawled name before he read again the pertinent sections. Then he tossed the letter into the flames and watched it burn to ash.

Nazenby didn't want him to warn Audley. He didn't know if he should follow that plan. He knew nothing about the cryptographer. He might be bookish and skittish. Or he could be up to any game and capable of defending himself.

Audley didn't even know who Toby was. He needed to meet the cryptographer and get a reading on his character.

That was a plan for tomorrow. For tonight?

He sat in his chair and poured more whisky to help drown the memories of his last day in Paris.

.~.~.~.

London

Stellensgard stood with hands behind his back. "The information that you requested is difficult to access. And my questions about Master A may have aroused suspicions."

Poulaine wanted to curse. Instead, he glanced at Saultsein and let that man ask the necessary questions. "Can you be more certain than *may have*?"

"I believe that I have aroused suspicions. Perhaps I asked the wrong person yesterday. The head of my department called me into his office after the noon hour and lectured me about looking for information beyond my duties. He informed me that I was bound by secrecy, not just outside the office but inside."

"You work with people who have their noses stuck in documents all day. I would think they would be eager to talk whenever a break is possible. They will hardly look for a spy in their midst."

Stellensgard only looked gloomy. "In the translation office, yes, we are all eager to talk, but we usually discuss foreign plays and novels and philosophers. Never the documents that we have seen. I believe that it was my visit to the file repository that raised the most questions."

"Did they ask if you were looking for anything specifically?"

"I told them that I had run across a few names in a document that I was translating and wanted to check the names against a previous document that I had translated. My department head is familiar with my memory. He did not think that was the problem. It was my questions and comments to the man in the file repository."

Losing patience, Poulaine inserted himself. "Did you discover anything?"

"I stayed at the file repository all morning. That is another reason I may have raised suspicions. I believe Master A resides in a small village in York. He left London early last fall for a property he owns on the moors. East of York."

"The village?" he demanded.

"Little Houghton."

Saultsein lifted a sole finger on his wine glass as he drank. Poulaine knew the signal of old.

Little Houghton. The same location as the artist Eugene DesChamps. The strands of the web were coming together. "Anything on the woman?"

"Not yet. I think I was close to the correct file, but I had already spent too much time. I will go again in a few days."

"You will go tomorrow morning," the Frenchman insisted. "I need this information. Tell your superior that you have encountered an unusual set of names that might be a code."

"They will want to know—."

"Tell them that you will not explain until you have proof. That should silence them and get you immediate access to the files. Do you understand?"

"Yes, sir, I do. But I will need something to tell them when I do not have an unusual set of names. And they will want to see the document that piqued my interest."

"You can forge such a document tonight."

"And the set of names?"

"Must I do everything for you?" Poulaine huffed. "Surely you have a gazetteer. You English have unusual place names. Bury St. Edmunds. Coffinswell. Lower Slaughter. Have you no surnames that seem equally strange that you can associate with such a place?"

"We do, but—."

"Forge your document tonight. You brag of your memory. Select a true name from a document that you have translated and place it in this document. Add in your fake names along with such a place as Lower Slaughter."

"Will that be enough?"

Even Saultsein huffed this time. "You have no imagination, fool. If you connect these names to a place in Paris itself, a place that seems to have no connection to England but would be of great importance to the French military, then you have created a false trail that should survive long enough to lift suspicions about your visits to the repository."

"And when everything falls apart?"

"You will be long gone. Do your job for Mr. Poulaine, and I will ensure that you move on to another position with all dispatch."

Poulaine didn't look at Saultsein. He knew his host's meaning of the word *dispatch*. This *imbecile*, however, would not know. He expected a reward.

"Do this, and return here tomorrow night with the information that my guest needs."

"As you wish." But Stellensgard didn't obey the obvious dismissal in Saultsein's words. "I did find more information for you, Mr. Salsby. I wasn't expecting to find it so easily, but it fell into my hands just before I left." He paused, wringing drama from his words.

"And?"

"John James from the file repository sent the name to me. He is the man who directed me to the correct documents this morning. I let him know I would be monetarily grateful for any personal information that he could give me. And he sent the name of Master A!"

His thrilling tones had no effect upon Saultsein. "Monetarily grateful? You have bribed him. How do you know this information he sent is accurate? It could be a plant."

"I visited a friend of mine at the *Times*. He confirmed that the name given to me and the location I had found matched up."

"Another bribe?"

"He's a friend. He thinks we were just talking about a scholar who had worked at Somerset House on scientific documents. He does not know the types of documents."

"You say many words, Stellensgard. You have information of vital importance," Poulaine's composure masked his anger. Saultsein glanced at him then quickly away, "but you have yet to tell us the name of Master A."

A bead of sweat appeared on Stellensgard's brow. "I had no opportunity."

"You have opportunity now. Tell us."

"Audley."

"That is all?"

"Col. Charles Audley. My reporter friend gave me his whole name. Col. Charles Audley, living at Ridings in Little Houghton, Yorkshire."

Poulaine leaned back. He flicked a glance at his compatriot then rang the bell. "This is good information, Stellensgard. Speak to Mac. He will give you the money needed for your friend in the file repository. Do not forget your task for this evening: the forged document. I do not need to remind you to burn all your practice documents."

"No, Mr. Salsby, you don't need to remind me."

"And in the morning?"

"I'm to go to the file repository again and look for the name Mr. Poulaine wants. Both names, in fact."

"Three names," his handler reminded. "Eugenie de la Croix. Keiran Delaney. Jean Louis Jettere."

"Oh."

"Oh?"

"I forgot, Mr. Salsby. That's how I knew I was close to the correct file. Three names but only two people."

Poulaine leaned forward. "Delaney and Jettere are the same person."

Stellensgard gaped then recovered. "If you knew this, why did you ask me to look for two people?"

The door opened. Mac appeared. Poulaine did not even look at the incomer as he said, "I did not know it until this moment." He looked again at Saultsein, who motioned to the burly guard.

The guard ushered Stellensgard out of the room. The door closed on the informant's request for a hundred pounds to pay off a bribe.

Saultsein waited on Poulaine, calmly sipping his wine, and Poulaine waited until the footsteps descended to the ground floor. Then he looked at his host. "He has to die and quickly. And his reputation will need to be ruined. This reporter—."

"Will die with him. Trust me, Mac knows how to stage a scene to keep their deaths from blasting through the newspapers. I will set Mac to the task as soon as Stellensgard produces the information associated with your names. I will regret losing Stellensgard. He did well in a short amount of time."

"Only by involving two other people, one of which will have taken money. That man must also die."

"Mac will get the information from him before. He will not be easy to replace."

"But he can be."

"True. Replacements can always be found. Now, when he mentioned Little Houghton, I signaled you. I know this place. I have a man in place there. It is the home village of Josette Sourantine."

"Why should I know this woman's name?"

"You shouldn't—except that she is the reason Claude Thierry is in prison and Robert Le Brun was arrested and executed."

"You are going to move against this Sourantine woman?"

"She is currently untouchable. She is married to Lord Giles Hargreaves, second son of the Marquess of Grasmere. I have not yet determined how to move against her, but I shall. And I will move against her family. Her father was an *émigré*, a *chevalier* of some sort. They will regret abandoning Mother France."

Poulaine allowed himself a bit of amusement. "It is not a holy war, Saultsein."

The man grimaced. "And is your pursuit of this de la Croix woman not a holy war to you?"

"She escaped me once. She and Jettere. People do not escape me."

"Ah, a matter of pride. Pride falls, *mon ami*."

"I will not fall. Now, about the man you have in place there."

. ~ . ~ . ~ .

Poulaine lifted the wine he had brought and clinked it against

Reilly's beer bottle. "Little Houghton."

"And you're celebratin' that little name for what reason? Where is it?"

"East of York. You can find it on a postal map as I did."

"Are you saying Delaney is there?"

"Col. Charles Audley is there, and I believe the man who disguised himself as Keiran Delaney is there as well. All signs point to it. And you should know this: Delaney and Jean Louis Jettere are the same person."

"Never knew a Jettere. All I need to know is Delaney. I suppose you don't want me to kill Delaney on sight."

"Help me get Audley, and then you can have Delaney."

"Right then. Audley is in Little Houghton. Villages are hard to get into. Few places to hide except way out in the country. Only a few people, so strangers get noticed."

"You will have a reason to be in the village. You are going to take over a job. As a gardener. You know how to keep a garden, do you not?"

"I ain't dug a hole since I walked away from my ma telling me to do just that. But I'll do it to get Delaney. You know this job is waiting?"

"I have a contact here in London who has a man in place there."

"A village in Yorkshire? Who's there that's so important—besides this Audley man?"

"That need not concern either of us."

As Poulaine's carriage rolled away from Reilly's lodgings, he rubbed his hands together. The net was beginning to close. He would have to cast another one to catch de la Croix. Nevertheless, the bribes he had paid that allowed him to come to England were reaping the rewards he had so long desired.

Chapter 8 ~ Thursday, 12 March 1812

Little Houghton

Just as Toby's mouth covered Melly's, raindrops plopped onto them.

She jerked back with a squeal. "Hurry! No, Toby." She batted his hands away and began scooping the remains of their picnic into the basket.

"We'll be soaked before we reach any kind of shelter." He offered what he considered reasonable logic for a spring-time picnic on the edge of the moors.

"No. I refuse to accept that. Jenny's cottage is nearby. We can shelter there. Didn't I point it out to you on the way here?"

"I wasn't listening to you talk about your female friends." He shook out the cloth used for their table and wadded it up.

"You mean you ignored me."

He glanced at her. She didn't sounded perturbed. As she snatched the cloth from him and stuffed it into the basket, she didn't look perturbed, only anxious. She watched the sky. The heavy cloud that had kissed them with rain was rolling past. Other clouds crowded behind it, but bright blue peeked through.

"The rain's stopped."

"Not for long. Oh, this was a stupid picnic. I should never have let you persuade me."

"You said a picnic was an excellent idea."

She stopped hurrying and gave him her attention. "I wanted to spend some time with you alone. A picnic did sound like an opportunity for that. We could eat a little and talk a little and—and kiss a little. Yorkshire, however, does not cooperate for picnics in March. We will be freezing before we make it back home."

"Where is your friend's cottage? Along to that twisted tree then across the rise to the path, and it's tucked against a stand of trees."

"Toby! You *were* listening to me!" She linked their arm. "I wanted to see Jenny anyway. I understand that Col. Audley visited her, and then she went over to his house, and now she has visited him twice this week."

"That seems a little convoluted."

"It does, doesn't it? I think Col. Audley will make a run for Jenny."

As they reached the cart, the rain started up again. Ice pellets struck them as they climbed into the cart. The horse shook itself and tossed its head when Toby snapped the reins, but it set off at a good pace. Toby worried about the ice, but it soon changed to rain. By the time they reached the path, the moisture had shifted to a fine mist that soaked everything possible and then more.

Once on the path, Toby risked letting the horse have its head and shrugged out of his coat. He wrapped it around Melly. She clutched it with shaking fingers. "Thank you. I am freezing."

The rise of the hill seemed minor compared to the upswell of the moor. The wind hit them when they crested the hill, adding to their misery. Beyond the hill, sheltered by a stand of trees stood a greystone cottage with a few outbuildings scattered behind it. Lights in the cottage windows beckoned. The wind swept smoke away from the two chimneys on either end of the roof.

Toby glanced at Melly. Like a miserably wet cat, she huddled in his coat. Her hair streamed in wet rivulets. She shivered, and the rising wind that drove the rain added its danger. "Nearly there," he said, and she looked up, saw the cottage, and nodded. "A hot fire and hot tea with whiskey. If your friend is there and not off visiting Col. Audley again."

"Jenny will be there," she said, her teeth chattering on the occasional word. "Even if she is not, her maid will still let us warm by the fire. You will have to forego your whisky, though. Jenny doesn't drink it."

"She doesn't run a proper English home then."

"She's not English. She's French. Cognac for you, sir, not whisky, and a simple sherry will be my tipple."

With an eye on the clouds building from the west, Toby set the cart onto the path. They jolted over rocks and ruts and splashed through rivulets. The deep purple sky warned of more than rain. The horse shook its head but gamely kept up its speed. They crossed the distance in good time.

He jolted the cart to a stop and didn't care what his London friends would say about his driving. He jumped from the cart and helped Melly out, guiding her to the front door. He pounded on it.

A maid opened the door, and Toby propelled Melly inside. The warmth felt palpable.

"Miss Ratcliffe!" the maid said, sounding horrified.

"Is Jenny here? Mrs. DesChamps?

"She's painting."

"Can you get Jamie to put up the horse and cart? We'll find our way to Jenny."

"Yes, Miss. Oh, Miss, you're soaked."

"A half-hour before the fire and a hot tea will set me to rights, Clarrie." The maid hurried away, and Melly gave Toby an up-and-down look. "Ready to meet my good friend?"

"I will have to be, won't I?" He followed as she opened the door to a side room.

"Jenny, I've brought my friend to meet you. Toby and I have been caught in the rain. Don't be too shocked."

The woman stood before an easel. A paint-spattered smock concealed her form. As she turned, he saw dark hair, dark eyes, then a face unchanged by the past six years. A woman he knew. A woman he had sworn was dead.

Eugenie de la Croix.

Only she was Eugenie DesChamps here.

And Nazenby, curse him, must have known it. Just as he knew that Toby believe Eugenie was dead.

How long had Nazenby known she lived?

Where had she been since Paris? Who had sheltered? How long had she lived in England? How long had she lived here, in Little Houghton?

The questions kept coming, but he would not get any answers soon.

"Toby, may I present my good friend Mrs. Eugenie DesChamps. Jenny, this is Tobias Kennit."

Paintbrush and palette still in her hands, the French double agent curtsied. "M'sieur Kennit."

He squinted. "Eugenie DesChamps? DesChamps?"

"Yes, I told you, Toby."

He glanced at Melly then back to the Frenchwoman. He wouldn't let her gloat over his shock. He certainly wouldn't let her think she would face no repercussions for letting him believe that she was executed. "She looks like someone I knew in Paris. But you can't be her. She's dead."

Eugenie winced. He wondered if she would reveal the truth to her friend. She opened her mouth to speak, but Melly said, "I sense a tragic love story in your past, Toby."

"Not my tragic love story. It belongs to someone else."

The Frenchwoman had set aside her palette and wiped her brush on a rag. "Melly, you must change. Your gown——."

"I am soaked through," his innocent love declared. "I hope to borrow one of your gowns."

"*Mais oui, bein sur.* Clarrie will help you. And M'sieur Kennit, he may warm here beside the fire. I think my gardener has a clean shirt he may borrow as well. Let me ask." She hurried from the room.

Coward. He wanted her to answer his questions. He wanted her to explain where she had been.

Most of all, he wanted to know how she had escaped the Bastille.\

Or who had died in her place.

Melly touched Toby's arm. "You are scowling, Toby. Don't frighten her. I do not know her whole story, but she had several difficult years before she came here."

"She's been here long?"

"Two years. Eugenie smiles much more now than when she first arrived. I never asked about her past, and she never speaks of it. Does she look so much like the woman you knew in Paris?"

"They could be sisters. Twins," he added with an ironic twist. *Eugenie smiles much more now.* She hadn't smiled at him, not at all. What lies would she tell him? "You're shivering," and he wrapped an arm around her waist and drew her close. "You need to change."

Melly snuggled close. "You are a furnace," she chuckled, but she still shivered.

Toby rubbed her back. Over her head, he stared at the canvas, a study of the moors with storm clouds roiling above. And he scowled as he worked through his memories and reconciled them with the present.

Eugenie de la Croix had become Eugenie DesChamps. Jenny DesChamps, a woman who had charmed the people of Little Houghton as easily as she had charmed visitors to her *maison* in Paris.

Eugenie smiles much more. She had smiled in Paris, a bright smile that came easily when in company. When Louis Langley had introduced his young bride, she had smiled widely and chattered effortlessly with the young French officer Jean Louis Jettere, recently returned from Spain. Then Louis revealed to his wife that Jettere had a second identity as Keiran Delaney. Seated beside her husband, a man more than twice her age, her smile had faltered. Her dark eyes remained intent. She had had no comment to make.

Toby learned that she was more than part of Louis Langley's masquerade as Louis Langlais de la Croix. Together, they created the false appearance of a recently married couple, a middle-aged dilettante who had survived the Reign of Terror and a young lady who had cast off her noble origins to join the other *citoyens bourgeois* in Paris. They belonged to the *riches nouveaux* who came to the capitol to exploit the other newly elevated who crowded into the positions vacated by the aristocrats. All of Paris, including government officials and military officers, found their way to the de la Croix residence near *La Place St. Germain.*

His own masquerade, as Keiran Delaney with disaffected Irish rebels stationed in Paris and as Capitaine Jean Louis Jettere, one of the many officers fascinated by Paris *sensatione* Mdm. Eugenie de la Croix.

Yet as he worked with Louis and Eugenie, he gradually realized that her welcoming smiles for all actually masked a solemn young woman. She never shared anything of her past. Her only focus was her husband's mission. A mission she adopted so completely that when Langley had died, she continued working with Kennit, still believing him to be an Irishman named Keiran Delaney disguising himself as Jean Louis Jettere.

Then their spying game crashed down.

A man Eugenie had distrusted but always greeted with a smile came to the *appartement* that Toby maintained as Keiran Delaney. The soldiers marching behind him made evident Poulaine intended to arrest him. He had escaped across the roof. When he reached *La Place St. Germain,* more soldiers filled the street before her residence. He broke into an attic window and ventured belowstairs only to encounter men searching the house. He retreated before they saw him.

But he hadn't left. From an adjacent rooftop, he watched until he saw Eugenie taken from the house. She screamed as the soldiers placed her in a cart. Servants had soon joined her in the tumbrel. Then Poulaine had spotted him and raised a hue and cry. Toby never knew what had led the French agent to look at the rooftops and spot him leaning over the parapet. He had fled the street and then the district. When he realized soldiers waited at his other lodging, the one he kept as Jean Louis Jettere, he fled the city itself, heading north.

But Eugenie haunted him. Remembering the memorized map of the Bastille, he had doubled back to free her—too late.

Yet Poulaine hadn't executed her. What poor woman had taken Eugenie's place?

The door opened, and the Frenchwoman returned with white cotton in hand. "Clarrie did the laundry just yesterday. She ironed Jamie's shirts this morning, so this is clean." She handed it to Toby without meeting his eyes and turned to her young friend. "Come, Melly. Clarrie is upstairs. A change of clothes, hot tea with a little cognac, and you will not remember being cold, *mon amie.*"

When the door closed again, Toby stripped off his soaked jacket and shirt and yanked on the gardener's shirt. The man was broader than he. The cotton billowed around his torso. He tucked it into his breeches and did up his fall. Then he shook out his discarded garments and set them to steam dry before the fire. He added fuel to the fire.

How had Eugenie de la Croix come to Little Houghton? He might scare the information out of another woman, but Eugenie would never admit to being scared. He needed something drastic to force her to reveal her purpose here. *Is she a threat? Or is she the ally that Nazenby had hinted about, the one who will help me defend Charles Audley?*

Nazenby. Toby nearly spat at thought of the spycatcher. *Will I ever get the truth from that old snake?*

The door opened, too quickly for Melly to have changed.

Toby straightened and turned to confront the double agent he'd once thought an ally. "I thought you were dead."

She winced. "A necessary lie."

"Does Nazenby know?" At her decided nod, Toby crossed his arms over his chest. "He didn't tell me. Did he send you here?"

"I found my own way to Little Houghton. He does not employ me."

So, she was not the ally Nazenby had told him to expect. Or she still played a double game, one that she had had much practiced for.

"Melly is a good friend." She crossed to the easel and touched her palette then the cup filled with soaking brushes, and finally the sketch she had tacked to a corner of the canvas. Over her shoulder she said, "I was pleased to hear she had fallen in love with a Tobias Kennit. Does she know what a rake Keiran Delaney is?"

"Does Charles Audley know you are a spy? A double agent for France?"

"Never for France." She glanced at the door, not at him. "Please do not speak of this, not here. Such conversation is dangerous."

"Your maid is upstairs with Melly." He looked at the bladed tool she had picked up. "You won't need that knife, Eugenie. I am not your enemy."

"We are no longer compatriots. I left that life far behind." The palette knife clattered back onto the tray. Clasping her hands before her, she finally faced him. "What do you wish to know, Del—*M'sieur* Kennit?"

"You're styling yourself as a widow again." He advanced on her. Angry at her, angry at Nazenby, angry that he let himself be played for a fool.

She gave a Gallic shrug. "I am the widow of Louis."

"He told me that the marriage was a sham."

Another shrug. "Louis told me that it would protect me. It has."

"Only until he died. Then you took up with Poulaine and others. How many did you take to bed to get the information you passed on to me?"

Eugenie flung her head back and didn't retreat from his advance. "I am not a *putain*."

"No?" He grabbed her, hauled her close, and mashed his mouth down on hers. He punished her for being a double agent, working for English against her home country, working for France against her husband's country. He punished her for being alive, for letting him believe she was dead, for all the months he had wanted her and she had kept him at more than arm's length. She writhed in his grasp and kept her mouth closed ... and jabbed her knee up.

Toby shoved her away. She hadn't crippled him, but he knew she would resort to claws next. She wouldn't take any assault tamely.

Shame washed over him. No matter what she had done, he was a better man than that. He had never hurt a woman, not deliberately, not callously. He had never wanted to be that kind of man who did so.

He certainly didn't want to be a man who toyed with one woman while the woman he loved was out of the room.

Revulsion rose in his throat, for himself, for this situation. *God, what to do?*

Eugenie swiped her hand over her mouth. "How dare you! We never had that kind of relationship. I never did, not with anyone. I never let anyone touch me, let alone kiss me. That you would think—no!"

"You flirted with them," he retorted, though her behavior didn't excuse his. "Didier Poulaine visited you often enough."

"As did you! But I warn you. It is dangerous to talk of those days. I try to forget those days. That is best," she added with a decided nod. She cast her eyes upwards. "As it is dangerous for you to touch me. Or did you forget that your fiancée will return momentarily?"

"Your English has improved."

Her eyes widened. "*Tu es imbecile, M'sieur* Kennit."

"Mr. Kennit? It used to be Keiran," he taunted her.

Eugenie had regained her aplomb. "Keiran. Jean Louis. Now Kennit. You have many names. You will say nothing about my past, not to anyone, or I will talk to the Rev. Ratcliffe. He and his wife wish Melly to marry an honourable man. You are a known gamester and a rake. This is proof. I will not need to say much, I think." Hearing footsteps descend the stairs, she glanced at the door. "We cannot talk of this now. You have anger at me, I think. I do not understand the reason. But for now, you are the fiancée of my good friend Melly, and that *is all*."

The door opened, admitting Melly, an Indian shawl enveloping her. Toby yanked a chair around to face the fire. "Here, sweetheart. Sit here."

She beamed at him. "Your Clarrie said she will have the tea in a few minutes, Jenny." She propped stockinged feet on a stool and wiggled her toes. "I already feel better."

"I don't," Toby declared. He lifted her feet, took the stool, and rested her feet on his knee. Her toes felt like ice, so he rubbed to warm them. "Mrs. DesChamps and I have discovered a few friends in common."

Melly looked at him, looked at her friend, then drew the shawl a little closer. "Not good friends, I think. You were looking daggers at each other."

"Your Mr. Kennit is not certain if I am a *Bonapartiste* or not. I have assured him that I have never supported Napoleon or this new version of the French government, and I never will. He will take some convincing, I think. I live a quiet life here in Little Houghton, *M'sieur*. I do not travel often. I do not have guests who visit."

He ignored her. "Your father, Melly, will have my hide for letting you become so wet and chilled."

"I am not an invalid, Toby."

The maid interrupted with the tea. Eugenie poured, adding a splash of cognac to Melly's cup. She added a larger splash to her own. Then she handed the bottle to Toby, letting him add his own brandy.

With Melly present, he regretted losing his temper with Eugenie. He especially regretted kissing her. Maybe that temporary insanity was driven by all those months of wanting her, when he'd been alone in Paris, with only Louis Langley as a trusted connection. He hadn't loved her, not the way he loved Melly. Lust, certainly. Loathing, for the *affaires* she had carried on with Poulaine and other men. Yet she claimed now that she had merely flirted, not engaged in intimate relations. And she had called him a fool.

He was. He admitted it. He could blame shock. He could blame years of guilt. He could blame a seething anger that increased with every year. He watched the Frenchwoman chat with her friend and tried to remember the reason she had once fascinated him.

She was still beautiful in that Gallic way of dark eyes and hair, a stark contrast to her creamy skin. Melly outshone her, though. Her violet eyes would crinkle in merriment and widen with her passion. When he tumbled her dark curls around her shoulders, she looked like the woman he wanted to spend hours with. She laughed easily while Eugenie had always had a deep solemnity. Toby had once thought her composure mysterious. Had she attracted him because she held herself aloof, out of touch as his friend's wife, still out of touch as his widow? The world had crashed down before he had maneuvered her toward any personal relationship.

She'd shown more passion in her anger at his kiss than he'd ever seen in Paris. Then she had resumed that imperturbable mantle that had once lured him, hunter sensing elusive prey.

Was that the only reason?

Melly chuckled, drawing his attention back to her. She had a sunny disposition that gladdened his heart. She welcomed his attentions and responded to his kisses. She had ardor that he'd never seen in the cool Frenchwoman. And he had risked breaking her heart with his foolishness.

The pang in his chest was unexpected and unusual. He didn't know how to classify it.

. ~ . ~ . ~ .

Toby returned after dark. He watched the maid close up the kitchen and lock the back door before stepping through the garden to a small cottage behind the main house. He scouted around the house. Light shone through uncurtained windows on one side of the front. He crept close and looked in.

Eugenie sat in a deep chair. A quilt over her lap, she read by lamplight. She tilted the book to the light and frowned over the text. The afternoon's upset had not disturbed her.

He had not lost the ability to pick a simple lock. He let himself into the kitchen. He moved silently across the planked floor. He eased into the hall. Lamplight streamed underneath the door to the sitting room. The doorknob turned easily, silently.

When he flung the door inward, Eugenie leaped up. And aimed a little pistol at him.

Toby grinned. "Going to shoot me, Eugenie?"

"Do I need to?"

He advanced. Her aim didn't waver as it tracked him to the chair across from hers. He sat without permission. Her eyebrows raised, but she resumed her seat.

"Your interrogation?"

"I deserve answers."

She pulled the quilt over her lap once more. She rested the butt of the pistol on the chair arm. "Ask what you must."

"Why are you here, Eugenie?"

"Here in Little Houghton? Or here in England? Or here alive?"

All three. His mouth twisted. "Are you still working for the French?"

"I never, never worked for them."

"I saw you give information to Poulaine," he accused.

"Only what he would discover soon anyway. Nothing that would betray the English. Louis taught me that much. Louis played that game very well, even to his last day. Poulaine came that day, did you know? No, how could you? You had gone to Marseilles. Poulaine visited the day that Louis died. He demanded to see Louis, and he stayed until Louis breathed his last. He came as a friend, he said." She hissed the words, anger for once overcoming her control. "A friend who would not leave even after the doctor drew the sheet over the head of Louis."

"Did you think—?"

She cut him off. "I kept Poulaine and the men like him guessing, thinking the information I gave was helpful and never aware of all I garnered by simply listening to their conversations." The cloak of control once more covered her.

"Poulaine eventually became aware. He arrested your entire household. How did he discover you were a double agent?"

"*Je ne sais pas.* I ran. I saw soldiers arresting everyone, and I ran. I did not offer myself for arrest so I could discover who had betrayed us."

"I watched the soldiers take into custody a woman who looked just like you."

She flinched. Her gaze dropped to the pistol she held. Light glinted on the chased barrel. "My cousin Annette. She arrived the evening before. We had laughed over her journey. We had laughed over a late dinner. We stayed up late talking. In the morning I had a message from a local priest about—it doesn't matter what drew me from the house. When I returned, the street was filled with soldiers, and Annette and my servants were hauled away in a tumbrel. Annette suffered in that prison because of me. She died because they thought she was me."

The story eased some deep-seated ache. He rubbed his breastbone. "Your cousin sacrificed herself for you."

"That is a guilt I can never escape. If I had had the chance, I would have killed Poulaine. I did not. I fled. I stayed alive. I managed to come to a place that I thought was one of safety." Those dark eyes lifted. Even with tears brimming, they stabbed him. "And because I am alive, you escape your guilt over my death, don't you, Keiran? Kennit, now, isn't it? Tobias Kennit."

"I am Tobias Kennit. Keiran Delaney was a disguise, just as Jettere was. Langley helped me develop Delaney as a disguise. He sent me to Italy, and when I returned, he had acquired a young wife named Eugenie. Neither you nor he ever told me anything more. Who are you really?"

"Eugenie DesChamps."

The name she now used. "Can I believe that?"

"Believe it or not, that is my name."

"An artist?"

"A very good artist of Yorkshire landscapes." She blinked away the tears that had never fallen. "A friend of Melly Ratcliffe, whom you intend to marry. If you do not ruin it with foolishness."

"How are you here in Little Houghton where Audley is? Unless you came to steal his ciphers? Or kill him?"

Her eyes opened very wide. Her mouth opened a little. She took a shuddering breath. "Audley? Charles Audley? He works with ciphers? For your government?"

She lied, and only the months of working together helped him see that. His former anger, though, had vanished as he drove Melly home. Exasperation replaced it. "Don't pretend ignorance, Eugenie. You can't lie to me. I know you too well. You know who Audley is. You know he is a master cryptographer. I don't know how you know, but you do. You must have tracked Audley to this village. You came here because it is his home. Now you have wormed your way into his acquaintance. A very close acquaintance if I am to believe Melly. Did you come here to spy on him? To copy his ciphers? Are you still selling information to whoever pays the most?"

The gun went flat on the chair arm. "I never—. I did not meet—. Keiran, you do not make the good sense. I have been here in Little Houghton for two years. Charles Audley only came last fall. How could I track him here when I was already here?"

Now she did sound like Nazenby's agent in place. He dared not mention that, his one ace in his hand, to be played only when necessary. Already he had played more cards about Audley than he should have. "I don't know," he said sullenly. "You managed somehow."

"You are deranged."

"Not deranged. I remember Paris. I remember two agents arrested by Poulaine who never left the Bastille. Agents you had just met. You had to have given them up to your spy master."

"I never gave him any agents. I only ever passed on information about shipments or boats crossing the Channel. I never worked for Poulaine. I never would, not after I saw him—. You should know this. Your spycatcher Nazenby should have told you about my family. I lost too much to Napoleon's government to ever support it. How high is this Charles Audley in your government? He is more than a scholar who creates ciphers, isn't he? What does he do?"

"You'll not weasel that from me."

"Did Sir Roger send you?"

"Did he place you here?"

Her mouth compressed, and Toby knew he frustrated her as much as she frustrated him. "I informed Sir Roger when I bought my cottage here. I have had no contact with him since then. I wish no contact with him. He is a cold man," and Toby nearly laughed at the self-possessed Frenchwoman calling someone 'cold'. "Poulaine—has he come to England? Is this the reason you question me about my connections with him? Is he searching for Charles?"

"Charles? Are you on a first-name basis with him?"

"Answer me, Keiran."

"Kennit. Use Kennit. It is my name, Eugenie. Keiran Delaney is no more, an identity that dissolved into the Seine."

She huffed impatience. "You said Charles works for the government. Ciphers, you said," and Toby winced. She was still quick. Eugenie never forgot a single slipped word. Once he had not only admired that ability but also depended on it. "Is Poulaine after Charles?"

"Nazenby said nothing about Poulaine."

"But Charles is in danger. Obviously, or you would not be here."

"I'm here for Melly."

"And also for Charles. Do not think to deny that. He is in danger? You must move him," she ordered, a decided command he had no intention of obeying. "You must move him far from here. To Scotland. Or Wales. Or Ireland."

"You know I can't go to Ireland. My identity as Keiran Delaney, Irish agent, was exposed. I would be *persona non grata* there. And Wales is out. That's my home. Is that the reason you put Ireland and Wales in your list, Eugenie? You want me to take Audley to Scotland?"

"You remain an imbecile, Kennit. You must move Charles. Pick the place for yourself. Do not tell me. I do not care where you take him, only that he is safe."

"No. Nazenby plays a deeper game."

Her eyes squeezed shut. Her lips moved with silent words. When her eyes opened, they stabbed him. "You will tell Charles he is in danger."

"Nazenby says no."

"At least talk to Charles. One conversation, and you will know if he can help in his own protection. You and I, we learned to read people. It is the reason we both distrusted Poulaine from the beginning." She looked at the pistol then carefully laid it on the table beside the lamp. "I do not care what you think about me. Please, tell Charles. He must be kept safe."

Toby shifted in his seat. She was adamant about the man's safety, and he could think of only one reason. The reason Melly had said. He didn't know if Eugenie DesChamps was any more trustworthy than Eugenie de la Croix was. His life had never been in danger until that last day in Paris. And she carried as much guilt as he did. More so, for she had sacrificed her cousin to save her own life. "This is not how I expected this conversation to end."

She looked up. "Nor I. I am glad I did not need my little pistol."

Only as he walked away from the cottage, finding his way back to his horse, tied beneath the trees, did Toby wonder who had betrayed them to Poulaine. For years he had thought she had somehow slipped up. Yet someone had drawn her from the house before the arrests began. Who had saved her?

Whoever it was had not cared that Keiran Delaney might be arrested.

.~.~.~.

Charles watched until the light left the downstairs room. Then it climbed the stairs to be muffled behind the heavy curtains of an upstairs window.

Striding along the road, he had seen the lone rider turn his horse toward the stand of trees. By the time he neared the road, the man was breaking into the back of the house. Charles had drawn his pistol and run to prevent—what kind of crime he didn't know, but he had expected to be a hero. He had not expected the intruder to sit down across from Eugenie and engage her in conversation.

He was ten times a fool to have watched through the window. Once he recognized Tobias Kennit, he was a hundred times a fool to linger to see what occurred. Had he expected them to fall into each other's arms? His heart had started beating when he saw the pistol she held on Kennit. His brain had started working as he watched their argument.

He knew Kennit's reputation. He had thought he was engaged to the oldest Ratcliffe daughter. What had brought him to Eugenie's cottage after dark?

He knew a Frenchwoman living in Yorkshire would have a mysterious past. She had all but admitted to spying. He knew Kennit had once worked as a spy in France. He could add. They began with argument; they ended with agreement. And they had made no move toward each other. Wary allies, then. What had they been in the past?

Charles knew he should have stayed at his desk. He should have created the next iteration of his cipher. He had a thick packet to decode, hand delivered yesterday.

But Eugenie DesChamps had proved a more intriguing puzzle, so intriguing that he'd thrown on a coat and walked to her cottage to—what? Talk to her? Kiss her? Seduce her?

Perhaps it was best that he'd seen her arguing with Kennit.

He was a thousand times a fool.

What would he say when next they met?

No one's past was ever quite in the dust.

Hands in pockets, he walked back to Ridings. Now that she and Kennit seemed reconciled, would they resume their past *affaire*? Was there a past *affaire*? Would the man leave her alone while he courted Miss Ratcliffe? Or would he keep Eugenie dangling?

What was their past connection?

Kennit was a spy. Had she been his contact? Or a fellow spy?

Chapter 9 ~ Friday, 13 March 1812

London

Stellensgard rocked on his toes, like a child with important news. "An unusual file, Mr. Salsby," he reported, although he looked at Poulaine. "A single sheet of paper. Five names, with a span of years written beside each one. Except for one name, the span of years covered a decade. The fifth name covered from 1782 to 1802. Those years included the ones you had mentioned, sir."

He paused and looked from one man to the other, obviously expecting praise or questions. Poulaine did nothing. Saultsein shifted in his upholstered chair. "Go on. Which name covered two decades?"

"That was the first name on the list. An Englishman, Louis Langley. A notation beside his name stated *in place as de la Croix*."

Poulaine leaned forward. "Louis Langlais?" he enunciated the name with a French accent.

"No, sir. Langley."

He leaned back, working hard to keep his eye from twitching. "I should have expected that. What else?"

"Beneath his name," he consulted a scrap of paper, "it noted *a pretense of marriage with Eugenie de la Croix*."

"Ah, you found her."

"That file is the only one that mentions her by name, sir. There are other names after hers."

"Let me guess: Etienne Foucault, Keiran Delaney, and Jean Louis Jettere."

"Delaney and Jettere, yes. Not Foucault. The other name in the list is Tobias Kennit."

Anger surged so quickly through Poulaine that he had to clench a fist to control it.

His host shifted in his chair, and Poulaine flashed him a look. Saultsein had seen his reaction to the name.

Saultsein sipped his wine. He licked his lips then remarked, "Kennit is a known libertine. I have met him myself, gaming at salons. My sources tell me that he just recently left London after returning from a visit to his estate in Wales."

"Where did he go?"

"I will have that information for you soon."

Poulaine jerked a nod and looked back at the informant. "Have you any other information?"

"I researched Delaney and Jettere. The repository has files on neither. However, an old file on Tobias Kennit does exist. It is almost as empty as the de la Croix woman's. Their names are on an otherwise blank sheet in Kennit's file. And—."

Poulaine, drinking his wine at a gulp, nearly didn't hear that hesitant last word. He lowered the glass and wiped his mouth. "And?"

"That paper at the back of Kennit's file, it had a later addition, in different ink, from '10. This is most curious, sir." He paused, drawing his portion out.

"Out with it."

Stellensgard jumped at Poulaine's growl. "Just a name. Well, two names, really. Eugenie de la Croix was written in the same ink as the first two names. Written in different ink, obviously a later addition, was the name Eugenie DesChamps."

I have you, Poulaine gloated. *After eight years, I have you. You thought you could escape. No one escapes me. You should know that, Eugenie. You saw me kill Foucault.*

"The lines intersect," Saultsein said.

Poulaine stood. "If that is all—."

"No, it's not all," Stellensgard said. "A town is also given beside the names of the two women." When the French master agent glared at him, he stuttered, "A v-village, s-sir. I f-found it on the map. Little Houghton."

This time Poulaine smiled.

After several more questions, Saultstein dismissed Stellensgard. He poured more wine for himself and Poulaine, then lifted his glass in a toast. "The second bird comes to your hand."

"She comes very easily to my hand." And he drained the goblet.

.~.~.~.

Saturday, 14 March 1812
Little Houghton

Eugenie watched Melly Ratcliffe and Tobias Kennit running the length of the cricket pitch. Melly's little brother counted the runs while two village boys scoured the knee-high grass.

"Unfair," Charles Audley said, taking his glasses from his nose to polish them. "Kennit's a rounder."

"A rounder? What is this?" Her head tilted as she watched Kennit dash back to the other wicket. He laughed as he passed Melly. "He runs in a circle?"

Charles's laugh rang over the lawn. With the bright sun and still air, the day almost felt like spring. His laugh warmed Eugenie enough that she would have sworn spring had come early. He had come up beside her but had said little and frowned as he watched the game. His laugh seemed to dismiss the disquiet cloaking him.

"A rounder is a cheat."

Her brow furrowed. "One can cheat at cricket?"

He chuckled as he touched her elbow. "He's a grown man playing cricket with boys half his size. He can out-run and out-hit and out-throw them."

"You were not here when the boys proposed the match. Melly and her sister are to be the handicaps."

"Miss Ratcliffe is the one that hit that ball into the grass. She's not a handicap."

"Is she also a rounder?"

"Definitely. But not—." He stopped. His hand dropped away. His frown returned. He faced the field, and Eugenie knew that whatever had smothered him when he first arrived had once more settled over him.

The ball came soaring back. The bowler caught it. A lanky youth with a shock of red hair, he whirled, but Kennit bounced into the crease and grounded his bat. On the other end of the pitch, Melly skidded to her position and waved at her cheering brother and sister. And the village boys suddenly looked deflated.

The Rev. Ratcliffe came up. Charles turned to speak with him. After an exchange of words, they stepped back for a quiet conversation, leaving Eugenie to watch the continued match alone. She wished she knew what troubled Charles. It could not be her own malady of guilt.

Melly was soon out, having missed her guard of her wickets to the consternation of Matthew, who heaped scorn on her ineptness, forgetting her successful hit of minutes before.

Fanning herself, she stopped beside Eugenie. "That was more fun than I anticipated."

"You enjoyed it."

"I did," she agreed, relish coloring her voice. "Mama will scold me, for I've gotten grass stains on the hem of my dress, but I do believe it was worth it. Matthew has been wanting to get his own back on those village boys since they trounced us last fall."

"Today the Ratcliffe team trounces them. Col. Audley says that you and *M'sieur* Kennit are rounders."

"We didn't cheat! But I will say that I do not think they were expecting me to hit so well. Matthew made me practice while we were in London. I told you about the little park at the end of the street."

She watched Melly watching her betrothed and felt sick to her stomach, remembering Keir—Kennit's painful kiss and the late evening *tete-a-tete*. Had anyone seen them, they might think to have stumbled upon a tryst. Had her maid come in while he kissed her, the gossip would have filled the village by this morning. Had Melly seen it, Kennit would have found himself riding back to London.

They were so very lucky that no one had seen that horrible kiss.

Guilt plagued her, though. She would have to admit her former acquaintance with Keir—Kennit to her friend. Melly was too quick— and Eugenie too far removed from keeping secrets hidden. Several times in her mind, she had slipped, wanting to call Keiran *Kennit*. There, she had done it again. She must begin thinking of him as Kennit. Tobias Kennit, she thought firmly. If she slipped, Melly would catch it. Then how was she to explain with deception already between them?

Two years of safety, and now this. Even one year ago, if Kennit had appeared, she would have retained enough of her old wits to prevent a mistake. This past year, though, she finally felt secure in her little backcountry village. She released into the Yorkshire wind all of those habits that were so deeply ingrained by four years of spying and six years of flying. Now, she must tug them back into place. And she would give Melly enough of the truth to keep any mistake from sending the young woman running.

She would avoid any mention of the kiss.

He hadn't intended it as a declaration of love. He wanted to shock her. He wanted to enforce his dominance over her. He wanted to punish her—for living while another woman died, for letting him think she'd been that other woman. His anger surprised Eugenie. She should have anticipated it. That anger was born in guilt, and that came from the deaths of Louis and Annette and all the necessary lies they'd told to winkle snippets of information to pass to the British government.

I will not tell Melly of the kiss, Eugenie vowed. *I will tell her of our past association.* That former connection must come out. Better to have Melly learn of it from her than be surprised and hurt by it later.

She slipped her arm into Melly's. "I wish to talk with you."

"Oh. Look! Run! Oh, run, Miranda!"

Eugenie waited until Miranda was safe behind the crease. "I need to talk with you."

Melly looked around with her big violet eyes that had likely won Kennit's heart with their first gaze into each other's eyes. "Wish. Need. This sounds serious."

"It is. A little."

"Is it Col. Audley?"

"Sh-h. We can talk over there."

There was the corner of the field where the mid-March sun blazed with the promise of spring.

As they walked past Charles talking to the vicar, Eugenie felt his gaze on her, as heavy as earlier. Had she looked his way, she would have seen a frown. Of that she was certain.

"You and Sir Charles! Your engagement would be wonderful news, Jenny."

"We are far from that, Melly. The days are early yet. Things have fallen apart before," she said with Gallic practicality. Things had fallen part, several times. Her little world had crashed down more than once. She had picked up the pieces and formed them into something better. First, when she left Saumer for Paris. When she fled Paris for Brussels. All those months in Groningen. And finally when she arrived in England and chose to settle in a small Yorkshire village.

"Has he kissed you yet?"

"Col. Audley is not the reason that I needed to talk with you, Melly."

"Kisses are excellent reasons to talk quietly." Then she noticed that Eugenie wasn't smiling. "You aren't happy."

"I have lied about who I am, Melly. I am not the widow you think I am."

"I know you fled France."

Her mouth twisted. "I lied about that, too. I did not leave France until '06. I came to England the same year that I arrived in Little Houghton. Before that, before—I lived in Paris under the name Eugenie de la Croix."

"You were married then?"

"A sham marriage. To an Englishman. To an English spy who went by the name Louis Langlais de la Croix. I helped him spy, and—and when I was nearly caught, I fled Paris. Eventually, I came here."

"You were a spy?"

Eugenie glanced around, but they remained well separated from the other spectators enjoying the sunshine and cricket match. "It is not wise to tell you this, Melly. The French government calls me a traitor. I am certain they have warrants to arrest Eugenie de la Croix."

"Is de la Croix your real name?"

"No. I am truly Eugenie DesChamps. I came here to regain myself. I *have* regained myself."

"Yet something is wrong. You would not be telling me this is something weren't wrong." This time, Melly's gaze searched around them. "What is it? Who is it? It has to be a *who*. Someone who has disrupted the even keel of your life."

Eugenie bit her lip then plunged in. "In Paris, I knew a man, an Englishman, who was sent to work with Louis my—my husband. He was truly a spy while I just played a double game."

"Col. Audley?"

"No." She watched Melly, hoping not to shock her too much. "Tobias Kennit."

"Toby? My Toby?"

She waited, reading shock then acceptance then sadness as each passed across Melly's face. She was so expressive, so open. No wonder Keir—Kennit, who had hated what they did—no wonder she had attracted him so strongly. Melly would never hide how she felt.

She didn't hide now. Her mouth twisted. "Then that rumor is true."

"What rumor?"

"Our kitchen maid Charity spoke to your maid at the shop yesterday afternoon." Her gaze remained on the cricket match. With two years' acquaintance, Eugenie knew Melly's inability to meet her gaze was a sign of her hurt. "Clarrie said that she had gone back to the house on Wednesday night. She heard you talking with someone, and later she saw Mr. Kennit leaving the cottage. I didn't quite think it possible, but Toby confirmed that he had been to see you."

"You confronted him?"

"I didn't have to. Curiously enough, he had already told me before Charity came back with the rumor. He said confession is good for the soul." Now Melly looked at her. "But he didn't confess anything except the midnight visit."

"I am glad he told you about his visit. Did he tell you that we knew each other in Paris?"

"He did. That puts you in Paris after 1800. You did not flee during the Revolution."

"A lie," she admitted. "A necessary one. As I said, I remained in Paris until `06."

"I think there are several lies in there, Jenny, not the least what you were doing in Paris when you and Toby met."

"What did he tell you?"

"I know he was a spy. Do not look so shocked. He didn't tell me. Josette Sourantine did. You remember her. She is Mr. Newland's granddaughter who went to stay with her sister-in-law in London."

"Her sister-in-law was killed in a carriage accident."

"There is a bit more to the story than that." Melly bit her lip. "I shouldn't tell you. Josette said everything is very secret. She didn't learn the whole of it until after her wedding. As for Toby, Josette learned of his past in a roundabout manner and unraveled the tangle. I may not have lived very many years, but I am not naïve, Jenny. He was a spy. He met you in Paris. That means you were a spy who must have worked with him. Or you worked against him."

"We worked together," she said quickly, not wanting Melly to think too badly of her.

Her friend's eyes narrowed. "You both controlled yourselves very well on Thursday. I didn't suspect you knew each other."

Eugenie bit her lip. She glanced at the cricket pitch where Toby Kennit and Matthew Ratcliffe were racing to score runs. The truth must be parceled out; some of it should never be told. "We were betrayed, somehow. He thought I was executed."

"A great shock to him, then, to see you standing in your studio. Why was it not a great shock to you?"

"I had already seen him, much earlier, here in the village. You remember when I questioned you about him? I had just seen him on the street."

Melly had not looked tense until she relaxed. "That makes sense. Were you lovers?"

"No!"

"You do not need to lie to me. I know he's a rake. He fascinates many women, and he's seduced dozens. That is the primary reason I hesitated to accept his offer. He claims that he gave that life up. I can accept that about his past as long as it remains in the past. But it would bother me, to know that my friend and my future husband were once lovers. I would always wonder—."

"We weren't," Eugenie said sturdily. "When we met, he thought I was married to the Englishman he came to assist. When Louis died, Keir—Kennit treated me with respect. He never even flirted with me. I think—he believed that I was a double agent. He didn't trust me. He thought I flirted with other men to get information from them." As she explained, her voice hardened until her last words dropped like stones.

"Keir—? What name did you nearly call Toby?"

"It was his covering disguise. I had thought it was his real name. I do not think I should tell you. He must be the one to tell you that name, and any other one that he assumed. These names, they are dangerous to repeat. We made enemies, Melly, enemies who would like to see us executed. As one enemy tried to execute me." She shuddered, remembering not only her narrow escape but the horrors that her cousin must have faced.

"You are safe now. You are in England."

"I fear that nowhere is truly safe, not as long as that man lives." She lifted her face to the sunshine. "I remind myself that I am in England, and the day is glorious, and I think we will win this cricket match."

"It certainly looks that way," Melly said and watched the game's progress. Eugenie thought she had answered all of her friend's questions until she said, "But I do wonder at Toby's reason for using the word 'confession'."

"*Pardon?*"

"Toby said confession is good for the soul. If he only talked to you—and I can understand the reason he chose midnight for your conversation. He didn't want to attract attention. If your maid hadn't returned to the cottage, no one would have known."

Eugenie's gaze turned toward Charles Audley. The sun shone on his hair, gilding the brown waves. He looked tall and sturdy, a man to rely on. He had held himself aloof from her today—when he did not forget to do so. Had another person besides Clarrie known of Toby's midnight visit?

"But Toby used the word 'confession'," Melly continued. "One only says 'confess' when they feel guilty."

"Not necessarily," she started to argue the point.

"Did he kiss you?"

"*Pardon?*"

"Don't lie to me, Jenny. Toby confessed one part. I want you to confess the other. Did you two kiss?"

Melly was testing her. How much had Kennit confessed?

"He kisses very well. I can understand if you wanted to remember something good from your past together."

"We were not lovers. I told you this. He *never* kissed me in Paris."

"But he kissed you Thursday night."

She had confessed without confessing. Scowling, Eugenie nodded. "He is an imbecile. I told him so."

Melly looked shocked. He hadn't told her. And she had hurt her friend.

She didn't offer the comfort of an arm. She didn't offer any comfort at all. "Will you listen to me?"

"Do I have a choice?"

"*Zut alors!* Always. Always and always. You always have a choice, Melly. If you want me to go away and never speak to you again, never call you friend, then I will do so. I will be aggrieved, for you are my dear friend, but I will obey. I have hurt you, *sans intention*. Will you listen to me?"

Melly considered her then nodded once.

"He kissed me. It was not *un moment de passion, tu sais. Il était en colère.*"

"English, please. My French is not up to this conversation."

Eugenie hauled back on the reins of her own temper. "He was angry. He wanted to punish me."

"Kissing is not punishment."

"He mashed his mouth on mine so hard that my teeth cut into my lip."

"Oh." Then, "Why was he angry?"

"Because for six years he thought I was dead, tortured then executed because I was caught while he escaped. Because he felt guilty for escaping. Because he abandoned spying. Because when I finally arrived in England, I did not ask Sir Rog—I did not ask his superior to inform him that I was alive. And those are just a few of the reasons he was angry. He is still angry. He confesses to you, but he leaves it to me to explain."

Melly stared. "Yes, I believe I would be angry, too. But can I believe you? You are a spy, just as he was. Spies have to be good liars, I would think, or they would not live long."

"I did not live long as Eugenie de la Croix," she rebutted. "They killed my cousin Annette, thinking she was me. That is guilt I live with."

She looked back at her betrothed. "I believe Toby still has a few questions to answer."

"And me?"

"You?"

"Are we still friends?"

Melly's brow constricted. "I don't know, Jenny. I have to think. I have to talk with Toby. And think some more. I am sorry."

"I understand." As her friend walked away, Eugenie looked at Charles Audley. He had no reason to believe her. He had claimed to trust her. Had she damaged his trust? His interest might not survive another confession.

Kennit had confirmed that Charles was a cryptographer, creating ciphers for the government. He would have a strong reason to cut himself off from a treacherous spy. Kennit would tell of his suspicions that she'd been a double agent, further damaging any trust Charles might have given her.

She should walk away. She should find an agent to sell her cottage and move elsewhere. The Lake District. The Highlands.

She shivered as a wind blew across the grass. It felt icy, straight off the North Sea.

The ice couldn't freeze her soul. But she felt frozen.

Snatching up her cloak, she swirled it around her. With a last glance at Charles, she started for the road and her lonely cottage.

.~.~.~.

London

Reilly's note crackled in Poulaine's hand.

I saw an old acquaintance from the time we spoke of. The name TK that you sent me. I believe he is indeed closely related to our friend Keiran. We don't have to miss him anymore.

The Irishman couched his words carefully. He would have made an excellent spy if he could control his violence against all things English.

Reilly confirmed what Stellensgard had reported: Keiran Delaney and Tobias Kennit were the same man.

There is a woman with that name you mentioned. Last name DesChamps.

That was a bit too clear for any spy, but the information ran a thrill up Poulaine's spine. Stellensgard's information ran true.

Eugenie de la Croix had become Eugenie DesChamps. The woman he had executed, Annette—the only claim she had made had been that she was visiting her cousin. He had traveled to Saumer. The village had no de la Croix families. But he remembered, vaguely, someone had called out *DesChamps*, and a man on the street had turned then walked back and joined a conversation.

Eugenie DesChamps, from Saumer.

He took the landscape from the wall and studied the name more closely. He cursed as his eyes failed him. He carried the painting over to his desk and dug a magnifier from a drawer. Then he carried both to the window. Bracing the frame on the sill, he bent close.

Yes! A faint line crossed the S at the end of the name, the flourish creating an X. She had flourished *de la Croix* in the same manner. She might obscure her name with the rocky ground, the same color as the signature, but it was readable to those who looked. Poulaine always looked.

Eugenie de la Croix had found her way to England and now masqueraded as Eugenie DesChamps.

It no longer looked like coincidence that the cryptographer Audley, the double agent Kennit, and the traitoress Eugenie DesChamps were all in the same village.

Chapter 10 ~ Sunday, 15 March 1812

Little Houghton

"You should be at church."

Melly folded her arms. "I am not charitable enough to listen to my father preach about God's love. I would have confronted you yesterday, but this conversation needed to be private."

Toby looked at the expanse of meadow. Melly had tracked him down. She used the word *confront*. He had seen her long conversation with Eugenie. The French agent had probably confessed everything.

This was not going to be easy.

"What do you want to know?" he tossed the ball back to her.

She looked startled only briefly. "Are you a spy?"

"I was. I quit. Back in '06."

"After you had to flee Paris. After you thought Jenny was executed."

The damned French witch *had* confessed all. "What do you want to know?" he asked again. "I will tell you anything. Just ask."

She caught her bottom lip between her teeth. Toby would have asked about his years as a spy or more details about his quitting or if he had ever been tempted to return. Melly, however, had a much more important question. "Why would you kiss Jenny?"

Ouch. "It meant nothing."

"That is what she said. She said you wanted to punish her. She said you kissed her so hard her teeth cut her lip. Why would you choose to punish her with a kiss? Were you lovers?"

What the Dickens? "No. Hell, no." Then he regretted the *hell*.

But she was nodding. "This event, it hurts me, Toby. I do not believe you are the careless rake that all the world has proclaimed you. I do not believe you do things without analyzing their results. This kiss was not a whim. Do you desire her?"

"No, of course not."

"She is very attractive."

"She can't hold a candle to you," he hastened to say.

"Do you wish an *affaire* with her? I understand this happens in London. The sophisticated of the *ton* accept *affaires*."

"Hell, no," he said again, because a simple no was too weak. "What did she say to you, that you have to ask these questions? I proposed marriage to you, Melly. You are the woman I want to marry and to love."

When she bit her bottom lip, he knew that denial and affirmation were far from enough. He hurried to add more, the plain truth, more of it than he'd ever given anyone. She would recognize any lie. She saw him too clearly.

"You know my reputation, Melly. You know that I go my own way. No one dictates to me. I've been in London eight years and never fell for any of the diamonds. One evening with you, and I'm hooked. I won't tell you that I didn't have affaires, but that wasn't my relationship with Eugenie de la Croix, or Eugenie DesChamps, as she styles herself now. I'm committed to you. I'm not interested in having an *affaire* with anyone, not now, not in the future. What did she tell you to make you doubt *us*?"

That last word was a good addition, for she blinked at it. He watched the hard glitter leave her eyes. "I thought Jenny told me quite a good bit, but afterwards, when I tried to understand your actions, I realized how little she had said about you, Toby. She said she knew you in Paris. She said you were friends, but no more."

He was going to have to tell things he had tried to forget. Not the worst things, thank God, but things that Nazenby had warned him to keep close to his vest.

"I fancied myself in love with her, when first we met. She was one of the diamonds in Paris then, the young wife of a wealthy *citoyen* who was rising in influence. When he died, I thought she would fade back into the countryside. Instead, not a fortnight after, she came to me with information she had gathered since his funeral. She had overheard some people at his gravesite, and she worked to find out the information. That's cold. And that's Eugenie de la Croix. Cold. Heartless. Oh, she can charm, but she doesn't care for anyone but herself. How can you love someone like that? I never could."

Melly studied his face. Toby tried to keep himself open, his eyes clear, his brow unfurrowed. He wanted to take her in his arms and convince her with kisses. Yet she had a rational mind well trained by her father. If he did manage to scramble her wits with passion, once she was away from him, that rational mind would turn back on. She would take out his words and study them until she had an answer that fit with the other pieces of her puzzle.

"You are clever, Toby. To criticize Jenny and flatter me indirectly, that is very clever. I suppose I am the woman who helped you realize what love is? If you wish me to believe that, you must explain the reason you kissed Jenny. For a man who had no feelings for her would not think to punish her with a kiss."

"It's warped," he declared. "Everything between Eugenie and myself has always been warped. We started with half-truths and half-lies, and we never straightened out our beginning. I should tell you about the younger Eugenie and the Irishman Keiran Delaney and a French officer named Jettere."

"Is this a half-truth and half-lie you are spinning for me? Who are these two men?"

"The covers I used when I was a spy in Paris."

But she wasn't surprised. "Jenny said it was not wise to talk of when you were spies. Yet she tells me, and now you tell me."

"No, it isn't wise. In fact, I was ordered never to mention those years or my contacts or anything related to that ... job. Eugenie and I can both be arrested for sharing even our cover names with you. If nothing else, that should convince you how serious I am. The French would pay thousands upon thousands of francs for us. I am given to understand that certain agents are still looking for us."

By the time he related his last days in Paris, with soldiers surrounding the house and blocking the streets, and seeing the corpse of the person he thought was his only ally, Melly was squeezing his hand.

"You never spied again?"

He hesitated. "I have been asked to keep an eye on Audley. I wasn't told Eugenie was here. I was told that someone here in Little Houghton would help keep Audley safe."

"Who is Audley? Why is he important? Why is he in danger? No, don't answer that," she hastened to add. "We stray too far from the point. I understand your connection to Jenny—Eugenie. I don't know what to call her."

"Stick with Jenny. To change the normal abruptly is to invite questions."

"One of your spy rules?"

He shrugged.

Melly touched his jaw, her fingers cold. He wanted to wrap her close, but the chasm still yawned beneath him. "I understand the reason you have a connection to Jenny. My father says the tightest bonds are formed from common danger. You and Jenny have such a bond. But Toby, that still does not explain the kiss. Nor can I believe a kiss can be punishment."

For answer, he snatched her close and treated her to the painful kiss he'd given Eugenie.

And his Melly didn't hang in his arms tamely. She shoved, then she readied her claws. He grabbed her hands and bent her arms behind her and gave her a second sample of teeth cutting into lips. Her head bent back at a severe angle. He hurt her with as much deliberation as he had hurt Eugenie, and he prayed that he would have the chance to make it up to her.

When he released her, she scrambled away. Shaky fingers dabbed at her bruised lips, the only mark he'd left on her.

"Now do you see?"

"How dare you treat me—?" She dodged, but he caught her easily.

"I never do anything without analyzing the repercussions," he reminded her.

"Yes. No. Toby, I didn't—."

His second kiss was as tender as possible, as sweet as possible. She resisted until he tongued her lips, then she opened her mouth on a sigh. He set out to seduce her then, and he didn't stop until she glowed in his arms, shattered by pleasure.

As he tugged her sleeves into place, he whispered in her ear, "That kiss was pure love, Melly."

She blinked. She shoved at his shoulder. "You—rake! You seduced me!"

"Not completely, Melly." She tried to break his embrace, but he kept his arms clasped. "Be still, my heart."

"I want to go home."

"And I want you to understand something."

"I understand how you earned a reputation as a rake! Let me go, Toby."

"Not yet. Did I hurt you?"

She looked mutinous, then she blushed. "I think my heart is bruised, nothing more."

"Your heart is not bruised from my loving, but from that first kiss. I will never treat you that way again, but you needed to understand. A woman can be decimated by a kiss."

Her eyes flicked over his face. "I do understand. I understand that you are unscrupulous."

"Lessons from my spying days, my heart. Put to good use at the gaming tables. Those days are over, thank God."

His words arrested her continued pushes at his arms. She leaned into his embrace. "What life do you live now? Seducer of vicar's daughters?"

"Husband of a vicar's daughter. Quite soon, I hope. Melly," He cupped her face, "I am the man who courted you in London. I am myself. I was never myself in Paris. It—warped me. It's taken a while to find myself again. You help. Seeing Eugenie—I think it took me back to those days. I don't know. I don't understand it. With you I am myself. I wasn't then."

"You are he and more." She sounded lost. "How many more? Who are you when you are Delaney? And that other man, the French one?"

"Just me. Spy no more. Rake, gamester: those are me. The man who wants to marry you. The man who thought you wanted to marry him."

"Yes, I believe that. How long will you want to play at being the husband of the vicar's daughter? That is a tame life compared to spy and rake and gamester."

"Toby Kennit did not choose those roles, my heart. They were thrust upon him. I became a spy in a misguided effort at patriotism. I fell into the second. And the third—I didn't care by then. My friend had fallen for a lady Captain Sharp."

"Careful. That's my friend Josette."

"Who became my friend, even though she saw the worst of my gaming. She put her trust in me. Can you not?"

"Her heart was not engaged."

Toby's hopes lifted. One arm drew her closer while his right hand slipped around to cup her nape. "Believe me, Melly. You not only represent all I have ever wanted, but also all I have ever dreamed."

She blinked. Those violet eyes looked lovely, shimmery with tears. "Is that the rake talking, the one who seduces gullible girls? How can I know?"

"Melly, Melly. I didn't kiss Eugenie because I loved her or even desired her. Do you believe that? Tell me."

"I believe that," she admitted slowly. "Unfortunately."

He stilled. "I don't like that word from you."

"It's the truth, Toby. You have swung me like a pendulum, anger to passion, unhappiness to confusion. I feel dizzy."

"If you arrive at happy and loving, I shall be content."

She blushed.

"Ah," he said and swept her up to convince her with more kisses.

"Toby," she warned at the first breath she had, "you have to let me go home."

He nuzzled her neck. She trembled. "My heart, you make too much sense."

"Yes. That is a sadness," she agreed. The words surprised a laugh from him.

.~.~.~.

After hours in the saddle, Charles looked between the horse's ears and saw Eugenie DesChamps' cottage ahead. He hadn't intended to turn the horse in this direction. He still didn't know what to say to her. He didn't know what to think.

At the cricket match he had watched her fervent conversation with Melinda Ratcliffe. He had wanted her to feel pangs of guilt. Yet when Eugenie walked away, alone, after the Ratcliffe girl rejoined her parents, he'd suffered the pangs of guilt.

Was it his business if she had an *affaire* with Tobias Kennit? Charles knew he shouldn't have been anywhere near her cottage on Thursday night. Ciphers whirling around his brain, he'd walked out to clear himself of numbers and letters and exhaust himself enough to sleep. He certainly hadn't expected to find himself approaching her cottage. The light shining in the front room window beckoned him. *She's awake, reading perhaps. We could talk. I want to tell her—*. He'd never finished that thought. He was fiercely glad that he hadn't, for when he had peered into the window, he saw Kennit sitting in a chair across from her. The man had leaned forward, intently speaking. Eugenie's reply had looked just as intense. Shock had scalded through him. He had retreated.

Kennit had left not long after. Charles wanted to knock on her door, ask her what was going on. He had no right to do so. That they hadn't made love was his only comfort. Scant comfort, he'd discovered in the remaining restless hours of that night. And the next night. And last night. The troublesome cipher solved itself easily. He sent it off to Sir Roger Nazenby in London. With nothing to engage his mind, he stewed over what he'd seen and what he could imagine.

If he'd been a drinking man, he would have drowned himself. He didn't have that recourse. So he walked or rode, driving himself to keep from concentrating on his destroyed dream.

This morning, when he'd looked in the mirror, he saw evidence of his sleepless nights. When he descended, his butler asked if he should send for the physician. Charles had looked at Tremaine, run the words through his head without comprehension, then sent for his horse.

He pulled his horse up and stared at the cottage. Smoke rose from two chimneys to meld with the slaty sky. Yesterday had felt like Spring; today, winter regained its hold. He toed the horse forward.

As he neared, movement at the side of the cottage attracted his attention. A man and a woman stood just beyond the broad chimney that centered this side of the cottage. The man bent, stood, bent again. His clothes were dun and brown, loose. When he straightened, his height matched the woman's.

Charles could not tell much about the woman. Swaddled in a cloak with a pink scarf over her head, she seemed to direct the man, for he moved farther along the cottage wall after she pointed. Then a wind gust tugged at the pink wool, lifting it away. She caught it back, but not before Charles had identified her dark hair and creamy complexion. The housemaid was Irish red and freckled. The woman had to be Eugenie.

He drew up his horse. *Do I want to talk to her? What will I say?*

The gardener pointed. She turned.

Charles prodded his horse forward. He watched for a sign from her. She looked back and spoke to the man. Then she walked around to the front steps. Standing before the green-painted door, she unwound the scarf. The wind tugged at her hair and played with the scarf in her hand and tugged at the hem of her cloak.

When he dismounted, the gardener took the reins and led his horse around to the small stable at the back. Charles just looked at Eugenie.

Her lips compressed. "Will you come in or just stand there?"

He hesitated. Not knowing what to say, he gestured to indicate the man who had now disappeared. "That man—he's not your usual gardener."

Her eyes widened in surprise, but she responded to his unasked question. "He is Reilly, a cousin of Jamey's. Jamey had to go to Liverpool for some reason he never quite made clear. Reilly brought the message and said he would work for me until Jamey comes back. I am not certain Reilly is the best replacement."

"You're planting already?"

"In a sunny spot, when the sun chooses to shine. I wanted Reilly to build a cold frame for early greens, but he seems not to understand what I want. Will you come in, Col. Audley?"

"I thought—." He cleared his throat. "I thought you were to call me *Charles.*"

"Will you come in, Charles?"

He stepped forward. She opened the green-painted door and led him in.

The hall that ran front to back was dark. To the left, her studio, was dark and curtained. The cursed sitting room on the right had a cheery fire. Disposing of her cloak on a hook, she went straight to the fire and added coal.

Charles shed his greatcoat and followed her, but he couldn't bring himself to come more than a few steps into the room. His gaze had landed on the chair that Kennit had occupied, and he couldn't pass it.

"Did you attend the service?"

He shook his head. With effort, he dragged his gaze from the chair to her. His sleep-disturbed nights were taking a toll on his concentration. "I was riding. Didn't you go? You always attend."

"Not today. I did not feel churchly."

How did she stand there and look so clear-eyed when dark desires had her in their talons? "*Churchly* is a not word."

"Pah, you English. You make so many words then tell me *churchly* is not a word."

He felt the frown furrowing his brow, but he couldn't smooth it away. He rubbed his fingers over the skin, and still the tension controlled him. "Eugenie—." He dropped his hand. He didn't know what else to say. "We need to talk."

Her gaze flashed across his face. "Me, I would say that the past couple of days have not served you any better than they have served me. I can offer you tea, Charles. And an omelet. My maid has the afternoon off."

"I'll take the omelet."

"Come." She brushed past him.

He followed her to the back of the house. The kitchen was also on the right side of the house. Tucked into the hearth was one of the iron ranges that handled a multitude of tasks, and its heat had warmed the room. Eugenie took a letter from a pocket in her gown and without hesitation fed it to the fire. Then she filled a kettle and set it to boil. Tying an apron around her plain dress, she reached for a bowl and fork then rummaged in a pantry and came back with four eggs.

When she passed him on a trip back from the pantry with spices mixed in the palm of her hand, he began to feel useless. "What can I do?"

"Plates and cups and saucers. Look in the cabinet there."

He found them after opening a couple of doors in the ceiling-high cabinet. He found flatware and napkins as well. He fumbled putting tea leaves into the tea ball then dropped it into a blue and white teapot sitting on the sideboard. By then she was pouring the eggs into a buttery skillet and the tea was steaming, ready to come on to boil. She found scones and set them to warm. He watched her work, and his heart ached for a domesticity that would never be. Not any longer.

She took the plates, turned the omelet onto one, divided it and slid the larger portion onto the other plate which she handed to him.

By then the kettle was singing. Eugenie brought it as well as her plate then returned for the scones and the butter keeper and a pot of honey. Then she sat across from him and draped a napkin in her lap. She looked expectantly at his plate and then at him. He picked up a fork and dug in ... and wanted to melt at the fluffiness of the eggs.

When he looked up again, his plate was empty and hers barely touched. "You were hungry, I think," she said mildly before she forked a bit of egg for herself. "Did you not eat before you went riding?" She passed him the warmed scones.

He took one. When she continued to hold the plate out, he took another. She set the plate down then handed him the butter. "I wasn't hungry then."

"Nor have you been sleeping. Me, I have eyes. I can see." She passed him the honey. "What is wrong? The ciphers, they do not go well?"

Arrested in mid-bite, he stared at her. "You shouldn't talk about the ciphers. Someone could overhear."

Her shrug was very Gallic. "No one is in the house."

"How many people have you told?"

"No one. Toby Kennit told me. He is here, from Sir Roger Nazenby. He did not intend to tell me," Eugenie shared the information as if it were not monumental. "He was—in French I would say he was *affecté*, or his thoughts *dérangé*."

"Upset," he supplied, his own mind re-arranging itself based on her knowledge of his work and her use of the English spycatcher's name. "How do you know Sir Roger?"

"I met him, many many years ago, in Paris. When I was pretending to be the young bride of Louis Langlais de la Croix, so that he would have a cover for his spying and I would have a cover for my revenge on the French who killed my family."

"You were a spy."

"Not truly a spy. Not the way you think."

"Not the way Tobias Kennit was."

She nodded and sipped her tea while his mind completed its re-organization and his mouth finished the bite of scone.

"You do not look as *exténué*, Charles."

Haggard, he translated. Yes, that word described what he'd seen in his mirror this morning. "So, you were a spy in Paris. Working against your own government."

"A long *histoire*."

"I'm not going anywhere."

She told him, briefly, while he polished off the rest of the scones. She poured another pot of tea as she listed off her family members killed because of Napoleon's government. She described her mother's death and her search for her missing little brother. And her encounter with Louis de la Croix, who convinced her to assist him as he would assist her.

"Louis Langley?" He gave the English pronunciation.

She handed him an apple. "You knew him?"

As Charles took the apple, he wondered if he were a gullible Adam for believing her. "From Oxford. He taught me how to decrypt my first cipher. He left around in the mid 1790's. I wondered what happened to him. He died in Paris?"

"He was in ill health," she said defensively.

A destroyed family. A spy. A fake marriage. "Why would you choose to become a spy?"

"I did not choose it. I tumbled into it."

"You pretended to be married to Langley. And you met Nazenby and then Kennit."

"Nazenby wished to confirm that I was not a nefarious woman seeking to dupe Louis. After that, he sent *M'sieur* Kennit. Only he called himself Keiran Delaney. He also masqueraded as a French officer, Jean Louis Jettere. He speaks French like a native."

"I believe his mother was French."

Eugenie shrugged, as if Kennit's background meant nothing to her, and Charles' dream kept re-building itself. "There. You know my sordid past, most of it, anyway." For a brief moment her eyes looked dark, then she poured them both more tea.

"What happened?"

"Que voulez-vous dire?"

"Something must have happened, or you would still be in Paris, working against your own country."

Holding her cup in both hands, she stared into the liquid as if it held answers. "We were betrayed. I do not know how or by whom. I received a message to leave the house. When I returned, everyone was being arrested, including my cousin, who had arrived late the night before. They must have thought she was me. We did look much the same. They executed her days later."

"And you?" he asked, trying to draw her out of the dark past.

Her mouth twisted. She sipped the tea then set the cup down. "I fled. Brussels. Dusseldorf. Groningen. And finally England and London and Sir Roger."

"You work for him?"

"Never."

The word was curt and cold. Charles tilted his head, trying to divine the reason for her animosity toward the spycatcher. "Nazenby mentioned that an artist lived in Little Houghton when I told him I was returning home. He said I would find the artist's work interesting."

She shrugged and sipped more tea.

"I saw you talking with Kennit the other night."

"Who did not? My maid heard us and spread it all over the village."

"Ah. The reason for yesterday's unhappy encounter with the Ratcliffe girl. And my own sleepless nights." When she searched his eyes, he found himself glad that he'd braved the words. "I would never have guessed two spies were in Little Houghton."

"And a master cryptographer."

"A miserable cryptographer. I was out walking, trying to work out a cipher, and found myself outside your cottage. I couldn't convince myself that the hour was too late for a visit—and then I saw Kennit through the window."

Eugenie flinched. "What did you see?"

"You two were talking. You looked like friends."

Her laugh was short, mirthless. "Far from it. You clearly did not see the little pistol I had aimed at him. I would call us allies, no more. Kennit thinks I sold out two English agents. He thinks I tracked you here to Little Houghton and will try to steal your work. I was here long before you. I am not spying on you."

"As you said."

"Why are you here?"

"Have you heard of a sweet spider trap?" Her eyes widened. He gave an abased grin. "I tumbled into one. Enjoyed it even knowing what it was. Alerted Nazenby. Moved on. Then Nazenby discovered a plot against me and ordered me out of London. He has people here. You apparently."

"I told you: I do not work for Nazenby. Charles, you came to your house directly from London? They will follow you here. This is a stupid plan. You should have gone where you had no connection."

"As you did, Eugenie. Only to encounter a fellow spy."

"He is a former spy."

"Miss Ratcliffe should be told."

"I did. On Saturday. At the cricket match. The day I walked home to avoid another conversation with you. The first conversation with my friend hurt too much."

"I wanted to avoid me, too, Eugenie."

"I will avoid Kennit. He thinks I caused my own cousin's death. *Il est imbecile*," she spat.

Her angry voice, her flashing eyes and scowl directed at Kennit reassured Charles more than the words. He felt like shouting or laughing, both of which were foolish, since she was obviously upset, more *dérangé* than *affecté*. He drained his tea then stood and came around the table to her. She looked up at him. He scooted her chair back, and she stood. *Foolishness be damned*, and he caught her in his arms.

She didn't struggle. For a brief moment she was quiescent, enduring his kiss without accepting it. Then a tremble rushed over her. A little sound broke in her throat. Her arms wrapped around his neck, and she opened her mouth.

He took advantage, more advantage than he should. He kept thinking she would stop him. When he kissed down her neck and across the swell of her breasts, when he slid his hands down her back to pull her against him, when he cupped a full breast in his hand, he expected her to recoil and slap his face. He only stopped when she said, "Ouch."

He had shoved her against the wall cabinet. He lifted his head.

Eugenie wiggled. "The door pull—."

Charles shifted her sideways. She giggled, which he stopped with another kiss.

His hand slipped under her skirts and up her inner thigh—and found the little pistol she wore strapped there. He laughed into her mouth.

She drew back.

"That's a pistol," he gave another laugh. "Left over from your spying days, Eugenie?"

"Of course," she said, ever the practical Frenchwoman.

Brought back to reality by the pocket pistol, he lowered her leg when what he wanted to do was explore his way to the top of her woolen stocking. She kissed his chin, along his jaw, while he tried to keep his wits. When she pressed her lips to his, and her tongue darted out, he convinced himself that one kiss wouldn't be dangerous.

Knocking on the back door stopped them the second time. Charles growled, which elicited another giggle. She pushed at him, and he stood back, watching as she jerked at her bodice and patted her skirts. She flashed her dark eyes at him, and he groaned and went to sit down at the table to control himself.

The knocker was the new gardener. "Will his lordship be wanting his horse anytime soon? The reason is, Miss DesChamps, that I'll be walking to the pub soon."

She glanced over her shoulder. "I suppose you should bring Col. Audley's horse. And it is Mrs. DesChamps, Reilly. Please to remember that."

"Yes, ma'am. I will."

"Bring his horse to the front, please." She shut the door and turned to Charles.

Her color was high. Her mouth looked well kissed. The gardener would have to be blind to miss what they had been doing. More gossip for the village, but Charles was fiercely glad about this gossip.

"Must I count it fortunate that he arrived when he did?"

"You should." His fingers flexed with the memory of her soft skin. "I won't." Her smile died when he added, "That man won't hesitate to tell everyone what he thinks we were doing. He won't be far wrong."

"First Kennit and now you." She pressed her fingers to her cheeks. "The whole village will have an ugly name for me by tomorrow."

"We can tell one great lie and one great truth," Charles ventured. Her brow furrowed as she tried to puzzle out his meaning. "The lie being that the man with you the other night was me, not Kennit."

"Charles, you are not really like Kennit."

"Did the maid see him? Only heard him? Then no one can challenge us about that."

"And the truth?"

"That you are going to marry me."

Her jaw dropped. A pretty little "oh" escaped. "Charles, are you trying to rescue my reputation?"

"I'm trying to propose."

She goggled. Then her French practicality surfaced. "It is too soon. We barely know each other."

"We've known each other since October. That's six months."

"A half-year is not long enough. No one should marry on such short acquaintance. Besides, we had our first private conversation only a couple of weeks ago."

He didn't mention that Kennit and the Ratcliffe girl would be marrying on a similar short acquaintance. "You want a betrothal of a full year? Do you think either of us can last that long?"

"Last?"

"Another fifteen minutes, Eugenie, and the gardener would have interrupted at a very embarrassing moment."

Her jaw dropped again. Her color flared brighter.

He thought for a moment that she would argue, then she shivered.

Charles remembered the way she had shivered in his arms, and he knew it wasn't fear that trembled through her.

He stood, looked at his state, and hoped his greatcoat would hide it from the gardener.

He had no way to hide it from Eugenie, whose eyes had rounded. "I will ride over tomorrow afternoon. You can give me your answer then." He headed for the hall.

She trailed after him. "I do not think this is a very romantic proposal."

He slung the greatcoat on. "Romantic will have you up against the wall again."

"Oh."

He grinned. "Yes, oh." Charles began to wonder if she'd never been with a man. Her kisses hadn't lacked experience. She had flared up like any good courtesan—or a woman first experiencing sensual pleasure. "Eugenie, how sham was your marriage to Louis Langley?"

"You do not need to be jealous. He was much older, and—."

"I'm not. Did you share a bed?" he asked, an oblique way to get to the truth.

"We did not have that kind of relationship. He treated me like a daughter."

"Ah. Anyone else have convivial congress with you?"

Her eyebrows shot up. "Charles, what are you asking?"

He sighed. "As politely as I can, I want to know if anyone has given you a green gown."

"A green gown? Why would anyone give me a green gown?"

Euphemisms had apparently escaped her vocabulary lessons. "Are you a virgin, Eugenie?"

"Why do you ask about green gowns and congress and—oh. *Galipettes*." She pressed her hands to her cheeks. "Go. Just go. I cannot answer such a question."

He left, wondering why she had brought up somersaults.

His horse must have thought him deranged when he started laughing a quarter-mile from the cottage.

Chapter 11 ~ Wednesday to Friday, 19 to 21 March 1812

Little Houghton

Reilly gave a jerk of his head. Poulaine touched his chin. The Irishman headed off, and Poulaine watched as he entered the pub.

He dealt with the innkeeper then walked into the public room of the inn. He kept his smile to himself as the innkeeper served as the host behind the bar. A swift glance informed him that neither wine nor spirits were to be had in this establishment. He accepted a pint and grimaced inwardly at the flavor of the beer even as he complimented the innkeeper on the brew. Then he wandered over to sit at a table beside a corner booth—where Reilly sat, his back to the room. The Irishman's pint was already half-empty.

"And?" Poulaine asked, his mouth hidden by his tankard.

"Yer right. That man Kennit, he is Delaney. I saw him. He's staying at this very inn, so ye better be careful."

"He won't see me. I can guarantee that. Did you find the woman? Eugenie de la Croix?"

"There is a Frenchwoman here. Not de la Croix. Eugenie DesChamps. I'm her gardener."

A crow of triumph swelled in Poulaine's chest. He kept it swallowed. The time for celebration would come. Not yet. Not until he had the traitoress in Bastille. He would remind her then of Etienne Foucault's betrayal. He would remind her, and then he would give her to the guards. After that, he would offer her an easy death—and then deny it to her. She would suffer. She must. He had waited eight years too long.

"I wish to see this woman without her or Kennit seeing me. Where does she live?"

Reilly dithered, but he agreed to meet Poulaine in a quarter-hour just beyond the cemetery attached to the church.

The woman's cottage was a three-quarter-hour walk from the village. Poulaine's feet hurt by the time they neared the greystone cottage with its painted door. His boots were made for paved streets and cobbled lanes, not rutted roads and tussocky hills. At least Reilly did not lead him up to the moors.

From the window of his coach he'd seen how the moors stretched for miles. A man could get lost on the moors. A man could hide his deeds on the moors. Delaney's corpse would not be found until the black vultures circled over him.

The clouds gathered thicker, and he groused inwardly that he would be rain-soaked before he returned to the inn.

As they approached the cottage from its rear, he remarked to Reilly, "I will need a road that leads directly to the sea. My ship awaits me just off Staithes."

"I can lead ye."

"I'll have two people with me. A man and this woman, if she is Eugenie de la Croix."

"Who's the man?"

"Someone that my government wants very much to control."

"And Delaney?"

"You can have him after you help me. Do you have someone who can serve as a guard?"

"Jamey's still around. He's handy with a pistol. Here, stand here, and look in the front window. She's in there painting. She'll move over in a bit so's ye can see her."

Poulaine waited, as still as an upright pole. The room he looked into was well-lit. Occasionally he had a glimpse of fabric moving, once of a hand reaching out to pick something up. He remained patient. What was a few minutes measured against eight years? Reilly shifted, muttered something to himself, padded back into the trees, then came back. Droplets of rain pattered down. And still Poulaine waited.

"Who's the man?" the Irishman asked.

"Charles Audley."

"The colonel?" He gave a low whistle. "What's he done? Is he a spy as well?"

"A cryptographer. He codes and decodes ciphers." There! The woman had moved to stand before the window.

Poulaine peered through the soft rain. Dark hair, slim form. In profile it did look like Eugenie de la Croix.

He should be able to recognize her in profile. He'd stared at it long enough on their return from Chartres, where he'd killed Etienne Foucault. He had wondered if she'd seen him kill the traitor. She had denied following him from the café to the surrounding farms. She had not acted afraid of him, but chatted idly about the cathedral and the village, the wine served with the *dejeuner*, her marriage to Louis de la Croix, a dozen different things over the hours and hours as the carriage rolled back to Paris.

He had not known for certain that she'd seen the murder until years later. On a visit to her *maison* in St. Germain, he'd seen a portfolio with a loose sheaf of paper. He had opened it and turned through the drawings, stopping only when he saw a field with a man standing in the center of it. Two paths through the tall grain had converged where the man stood, and something dark lay at his feet. Poulaine had withdrawn the sheet, folded it neatly, and placed it in his vest pocket. He vowed at that moment to bring about Eugenie de la Croix's demise before she told any authority about his murder of Etienne Foucault.

In two weeks he had set in motion the necessary forms to have her arrested. In another week he had approval for her arrest, based on testimony he had suborned. And in the fourth week he had stumbled on Jettere's duplicity when Reilly saw the man and named him Keiran Delaney, Irish rebel rather than a French officer. Before the end of that week, Poulaine set in the motion the arrests for the two traitors.

Yet someone had tipped off the woman. She must have left her home before the soldiers arrived to arrest her. By mistake, they took her cousin into custody. Jettere was vanished as well, fled northward.

He never had found Eugenie de la Croix's means of escaping him.

That was her profile.

Then the woman turned, and Poulaine drew in a deep breath of satisfaction. Yes.

"That her?" Reilly asked.

He rubbed his hands together. Turning up his coat collar against the increasing rain, he faded behind the tree and hedge. "I must remain concealed. We must move quickly. I delayed before, and both slipped the noose. They will not slip away this time."

.~.~.~.

Reilly demanded a day to get his man back in Little Houghton. With all ready, Poulaine followed the Irishman to the cottage. The maid reluctantly admitted them to the kitchen.

"She's not here," she said in answer to Reilly's demand. "She walked over to Ridings."

"What is this Ridings?" Poulaine asked.

"Manor belonging to Audley."

"Ah. You have your man in place there?"

"I said I was ready, didn't I? How long will she be at the manor?" he shot at the maid.

"She stays two or three hours. She's working on a painting over there. The colonel hired her to paint the view from his study."

Reilly swore softly. Poulaine had more patience. "When will she return?"

"I expect her back at three o'clock."

"We could take the both of them——."

"No," he interrupted. How much the Irish maid knew, Poulaine wouldn't ask, but he didn't want to add to her knowledge. "Too many people. We will wait.

A quarter-hour before three, the front door opened. Reilly surged to his feet. Poulaine motioned for him to be quiet.

"Clarry!" Steps came toward the kitchen.

Reilly positioned himself behind the swing of the door.

"Clarry!" The door opened. Eugenie de la Croix appeared. She saw him immediately and stopped. She started to back up—but the door shut. She looked left and saw the big Irishman. "Reilly?" she questioned. Then she looked back at Poulaine, and her whitened face gratified him. She knew the reason he was here. She knew the Irishman was leagued with him. She knew how futile resistance was.

.~.~.~.

For a brief second Eugenie considered snatching her little pistol from its hiding place. But she had only one bullet. Poulaine was dangerous, but she thought Reilly would be violent. Better to keep her pistol hidden. "I will not go with you."

"Ah, you do not dissemble. That pleases me. We have played a long chess game, you and I, but this is not Paris. You are checked now, with nowhere to run."

"I will not go with you, Poulaine," she repeated sturdily.

"You will." He unfolded from the chair and loomed over her. She lifted her chin and held his gaze. "I have a little bargain for you. You see, I am not here for you. I want your lover."

For a half-second she thought he meant Kennit because of the rumors.

"I am here for Charles Audley," he continued. "Did you know he makes ciphers? Complicated ciphers that our best people spend weeks and weeks trying to decode. Yet he cracks our codes without problem. He has become a hindrance we can no longer abide. I am ordered to bring him back to France. If he fights me, I am ordered to kill him. I would rather kill him—but my advancement depends upon his return, alive, captive to our will. You will help me, Eugenie, to get him to France."

"Never. Do you think I am a fool, Poulaine? You will kill him and kill me."

"I would rather deliver you to the executioner, Madame de la Croix. I think your lover would be willing to go to France rather than allow you to die. Together, you will ensure each other's cooperation. Apart, you both die."

"That is no choice, at all. I will die either way."

"You can live long enough to ensure his life, or die now. It is a *little* bargain I offer you. A few more days of life. The grace of a few more hours with your lover. He will continue to live—if you help me. I would think you would want him to live, yes?"

She did not need a second to decide. Alive, they had a chance. "Yes."

"Good. Come this way, Madame. My carriage waits beyond the hill."

.~.~.~.

The cottage was cold, the fires out and no lamps lit against the approaching darkness. Eugenie had said she was returning home, but she was in none of the rooms. Nor was the maid. When he pounded on the door of the maid's little abode, no one answered. Charles shoved open the door. The single room was as cold as the cottage and just as empty.

No. Not empty.

He walked over to the bed and pulled the quilted coverlet back. The hairs on his nape lifted.

The red-haired maid lay there. Her open eyes stared up. Bruises on her neck told the story.

Gorge rose into his throat. Grimly, he swallowed it down. He checked for the pistol he carried by habit inside his jacket.

What had Eugenie said? Nazenby had sent Kennit to keep an eye on him, to protect his valuable cryptographer from the French agents sent to kidnap him and take him to France. He knew that, but he had never appreciated the danger he was in.

Had the French agents come to Little Houghton to get him and somehow discovered Eugenie, a former agent working for the English against her own government? She would be a prize to take back for execution.

Charles ran for his horse. He could raise searchers at Ridings—but Eugenie wasn't lost. She was taken. Probably by the very men who wanted to kidnap him.

How could he put himself into their hands and still protect her?

Kennit wasn't at the inn. He was at the vicarage. When Charles burst into the sitting room, Kennit straightened up with a speed that no indolent gamester could have managed. But he wasn't an indolent gamester. He was a spy, years away from active work but his wits and reactions still sharp.

Melly Ratcliffe looked up from her writing. The vicar's wife held her needle in the air and gaped at him.

"She's gone," he said without preamble.

"She left?"

"Her cottage is deserted. Someone killed her maid. Strangled her."

Kennit moved then. He patted his breast pocket, and Charles knew he was also armed. "Melly, your father—." She was up and across the room without his saying more.

Charles stepped out of the way.

"How much did she tell you?"

"Enough. I have brain enough to figure out the rest. They'll want to execute her."

Mrs. Ratcliffe gasped. "What are you talking about?"

Both men ignored her. "They're here for you," Kennit said. "You're the bigger prize. They've been hunting you for six months and more, according to Nazenby."

"I don't care about my safety. Will you help? Or will you abandon her to them?"

"I didn't abandon her before. I thought she was dead. I would never have left her to Poulaine. I tried to get her out of the Bastille."

"That wasn't her. That was her cousin."

"If the French have her—."

"I'm the bigger prize. I can be the bait."

"Nazenby would never countenance that," said the vicar from the doorway. "Esmeralda, I do not think this is a conversation that you should be hearing."

"I've heard enough of it now, John. Melly, I think your father may need his horse."

"Then send for Alex Montague. We're going to need him." The girl vanished from the doorway, and the vicar turned back to the younger men. "Kennit is right, Audley. We can't risk losing you."

"Be damned to my safety, Ratcliffe," he ground, not caring that he swore at the vicar. "I won't sit in safety while Eugenie's in danger. I was once good in a rugby scrum, and you've seen me shoot."

"Nazenby will have my head if anything happens to you." Yet Ratcliffe made no other protest. "Very well then. The agents have found their way here. Mrs. DesChamps is missing, her maid murdered—yes, Melly told me. We have two assumptions. Either they see Mrs. DesChamps as a hostage to lure you out, or they have recognized her from her days in Paris."

"Or both," Charles inserted.

"Or both," he agreed.

"Either way, I'm the prize they're after. They won't leave Little Houghton until they have me as well. I am the best bait. Be damned to Nazenby's concerns."

"That's twice you've cursed in less than five minutes," the vicar observed calmly. "As a vicar, I must remonstrate. As a man—well, I would say that Mrs. DesChamps must mean something to you."

"We're going to be married."

"Ah. Two marriages in the offing."

Charles bit back another curse at the man's composure. He flung out a hand. "Can we stop talking and get on with it? We must find them."

"No," Kennit said, "we must find a way for them to find you— while we lie in wait."

"The beginnings of a plan," Mrs. Ratcliffe said. "It must be tonight, gentlemen. The cover of darkness and all that. A cliché is a cliché for a reason. You should not wait for daylight. Not only will you be spotted, but Jenny should not be left in their clutches that long."

And a new horror rose in Charles' mind.

"Tonight then," her husband agreed. "We cannot strike them when they take him. They will not have Mrs. DesChamps with them. She will be secreted somewhere, under guard. We will have to follow them in order to find her. That is the dangerous part. If they spot us following, they will kill Audley and her. Once they have him, they may kill her anyway."

"No," Kennit said. "They will want to put her on trial for crimes against the government. They will want to execute her. They won't kill her outright."

"Small comfort," Charles added, "but that would be my guess. Because of her father and her brothers, she worked against her own country. They will want to punish her."

"She told you everything, didn't she? She must trust you."

"As she never trusted you," he shot back at Kennit. The man acknowledged the truth with a very Gallic shrug. Charles turned back to Ratcliffe. "So, I am the bait. Where do you plant me so they can find me?"

"We need Montague. He'll bring his son. With Kennit and myself, that's four who will be armed and following. Any more, and they will spot us. Have you a knife for your boot?"

"They'll find that. They'll find my pistol. They would be fools not to search me."

"So, we will give them weapons to find. And perhaps you will also have a weapon they will not expect. How good are you with knives?"

"Decent at throwing, no good in a close fight. Better with a pistol. If you have a small one-shot—."

Ratcliffe shook his head. "We'll stick to the knife, I think. We wait on Montague, then." He looked at Kennit. "How long have you known I am Nazenby's man?"

"I didn't, sir. Process of elimination."

"I have a name for you. It came by courier this afternoon. Nazenby has found out the name of the French agent trying to track Audley here. Didier Poulaine." When Kennit cursed, the vicar added, still calmly, "I see that name means something to you."

Charles slewed around to listen.

"Poulaine is one of their chief operatives, sir. Big man with pig eyes and a broken nose. One of their best. Dogged in tracing information. Cruel in twisting it out of people. I escaped him by a whisker back in `04. As did Eugenie. I thought he had had her executed until I encountered her here. He's not one to forget, either."

Charles ignored their continued conversation. He wanted to pace the room, but that would only increase his agitation. He wanted to get on with the planning, but Montague and his son had yet to arrive. He did not even dare to stare out the window. He didn't want anyone to see him here, hatching a scheme to rescue Eugenie without getting himself and her killed.

Chapter 12 ~~ Friday to Saturday, 21 to 22 March 1812

Little Houghton

Charles came out of the pub and walked toward the village stable. He looked neither left nor right, but he flinched at every slight sound.

Ahead came the clip-clop of horses. Lanterns moved toward him as a carriage rolled along the street. He kept walking. French agents working fast wouldn't have the resources to provide themselves with a carriage at short notice. Ratcliffe had assured him of that point.

He knew Ratcliffe and Kennit and Montague watched from stations along the street. The younger Montague had remained at the vicarage with the horses.

Charles had worried about that lag of time, between the agents capturing him and then Kennit and the others following. Yet no matter how they had twisted the plan, they couldn't avoid that problem. The horses would be too noticeable, and horses they had to have. All of them agreed that the French would be hiding in one of the old cottages scattered around the district. Too many empty cottages. If he survived this, he would ensure those empty cottages were inhabited or were pulled down.

The carriage slowed as it neared him then jolted to a stop.

Only then did he realize the first flaw in the plan. The French had been looking for him for more than six months. Of course they had resources.

They had speculated the French agents had to be three in number, at least. Now he wondered if only two men were needed: the French agent and his local contact.

The man on the box lifted a musket from across his legs and pointed it at Charles.

The knife sheathed on his arm suddenly felt very conspicuous.

The carriage door swung open. A man stepped down. The lantern light reflected amber on the pistol he held. "Obliging of you to be alone, *M'sieur* Audley."

"You're French." A stupid comment, he realized. He should be impressing the man with his intellect.

"*Naturellement.* Please, come forward. I ask you to look inside the carriage." He stepped to the side to give Charles room.

Wary, wondering if his head was going to be bashed in, Charles stepped forward.

A single lamp inside the carriage lit the interior. A woman lay on the floor between the seats. She twisted around, and he saw that she was gagged, her hands bound in front of her with thick rope. A dark head lifted. Dark eyes stared. She tried to speak. If he knew Eugenie, she was demanding that he leave her.

"Have you hurt her?"

"*M'sieur*, that is not the first question I expected from you."

He couldn't look away from her dark eyes. "Have you hurt her?"

"Not yet. Her treatment depends upon you. Please join us, and I will not injure her."

She shook her head. Her loose curls slithered around her shoulders. She looked unhurt, her dress soiled but untorn—yet he remembered the maid, the only signs on her the bruises on her neck. A few bruises, and she was dead.

He hoped the others were running for their horses.

Charles climbed into the carriage. He sat on the bench facing backward. The carriage dipped as the Frenchman climbed inside.

When he reached for Eugenie's gag, the man said, "Do not." The pistol stayed steady on him. The carriage rolled forward. The man tossed iron shackles to him.

He didn't have to be told. He fastened them on his wrists. Then he looked at his enemy. "Who are you?"

"A man you do not know. My name will never be important to you."

"Your name will be important to me if you hurt Eugenie."

"Then I must become vastly important to you, for I will deliver this traitoress to the French courts for her treason. If you wish her to be well treated until then, you will cooperate."

Charles looked into those narrow-set piggy eyes and conceived a hate. The broken nose finished the identification, but he didn't call the man's name. Holding it back until the right time might give an edge. "I do not see any incentive in cooperation." He was amazed at his calm. Had he run through all of his adrenaline at the vicarage? "Your country wants to execute her."

"Ah, but she can go to her death pristine and unharmed or raped and beaten. Yours is the choice."

"Why me? I am no one."

"You are very important to us, Col. Charles Audley. You are the great cryptographer, the mysterious *Master A*. It has taken us months to track you down."

Only a handful of people knew that he was Master A, yet this man spoke as if Charles had never been unknown to them. "I won't help you. If you kill her, I will never help you."

The man shrugged. "Then you will die. All we care is that you no longer create ciphers for your government. You may live or die, again by your choice. My government wants you alive. They foolishly think that they can win you over."

"You don't think that."

"I do not care either way. My purpose is to deliver you and stop the ciphering. The execution of Madame de la Croix, that is a bonus, one that I will enjoy." He smiled in contemplation.

Charles saw a gold tooth winking at him. And his hatred grew.

.~.~.~.

The attack came out of an alley. Toby had only the glint of metal as a warning, then a bulky shape erupted from the shadows and bore him to the ground.

He fastened his hands on the arm swinging down with the knife and grimly held on. For a scant second, he thought his strength wasn't enough, then he heaved and rolled the man off him.

They grappled on the cobbles. The knife flew, skittering over the stones. Toby punched. His opponent didn't flinch. Big hands reached for his neck.

He heaved away, but the man had wrapped a leg around his. He hauled him back. He shoved his hand against Toby's chin, pushing his head back until bones needed to pop. He pummeled the man. Again his blows had no impact. The man's other hand came around and grappled for his jaw. He began to twist.

A body blow would be useless. He couldn't get an arm up to break the hold. Toby punched the man's temple. The twist eased, then started again.

Something dark loomed behind the man. Something glinted. A thud sounded. And the man collapsed on top of Toby.

While he crawled from underneath and staggered to his feet, his attacker was turned over. Toby craned his neck back into shape then stared at the man. "Who knocked him into a cocked hat?"

"I did," Montague said. He looked down at the man. "Do you know him?"

"Sorry to say I do. Irish rebel by name of Reilly."

"An Irishman Reilly was working as a gardener for Mrs. DesChamps this week," the vicar said.

While Toby goggled that Ratcliffe kept such close pins on the people in Little Houghton, Montague had a greater concern. "What do we do with him? Leave him here? We don't have time to fetch a constable." He looked along the road the carriage had taken. "We'll lose them if we wait much longer. Wherever they're going, I have a feeling they won't take the main road."

"Have to leave him," Toby said. His voice sounded hoarse. He craned his neck again and remembered those pops when Reilly had shoved his head back. "We need to get on the trail. Poulaine won't hesitate. He'll make straight for the coast. I know him of old. He'll have a ship waiting, and a dinghy already beached, ready to haul them out to the ship."

"We could leave my son to guard him."

"Begging your pardon, Montague, but Reilly will kill your son. Leave him. Let's go."

"I have to agree with Kennit, Montague."

Toby glanced back once before they turned toward the horses, and he lost sight of the big Irishman. The man was already sitting up, shaking his head. He would be on his feet in minutes.

He would know Poulaine's destination. He would be on their tails as soon as he found a horse. Or he would fly overland and get there before them—and warn Poulaine.

Dammit.

.~.~.~.

The carriage jounced its way over a rutted road for hours before turning onto a smoother road. Charles reckoned they were heading east. The first road would not have been the usual highway, but they had to be rolling over the common road now.

Poulaine never took his eyes from him. He had searched Charles and found his pistol and the knife in his boot. He didn't find the knife sheathed on his arm. That was the first thing that went right with their plan. His hopes began to climb.

Poulaine didn't deign to attend to Eugenie on the floor. His pistol rarely wavered in its direction, and it was directed at Charles' gut. If he had been alone, he would have attacked the Frenchman. Even chained, he stood a good chance. But he wouldn't risk Eugenie. He hoped she still had her one-shot pistol strapped to her leg. He had no way of knowing. He wouldn't depend on that weapon. Just his knife and his own hands and every dirty trick he'd ever learned while playing rugby.

Eugenie had closed her eyes hours ago. She opened them only when the carriage jolted over a rut and jounced her on the hard floor. Poulaine put his foot on her once. Charles snarled at him. The

Frenchman bared his teeth, the gold one again winking in the lamplight, but he put his boot back on the floor. The man didn't dare such again.

The carriage rolled into an innyard. The French agent pulled the curtains on either side, hiding the interior. The coachman climbed down, rocking the carriage on its axle. Charles heard the man talking with the groom who had run out. Irish accent. He didn't recognize the voice. When Eugenie's eyes opened, he thought she did recognize the voice. Then she retreated to her grim inner closet.

He wondered what she was thinking. Was she afraid? She didn't look afraid. He hoped she was angry. Anger would bolster her, especially if the four horsemen had lost them.

Not long after that, he caught the scent of the sea. In the darkness they rolled past a village he reckoned must be Staithes and continued on. Charles wracked his brain for a likely spot for a landing. It wouldn't need a large area, enough for a dinghy. Runswick Bay was too far and too well known. They were traveling north, for the sea was on his right.

They traveled a quarter-hour more before the carriage jerked to a stop.

Poulaine straightened and steadied his hold on the pistol. He smiled down at Eugenie. "Soon, *ma belle femme*, soon."

She glared and garbled something behind her gag. Still furious, still ready to fight. Charles wanted to grin.

The carriage door opened. A long barrel poked inside.

"You first, *M'sieur* Audley. Then you will help Mdm. de la Croix."

The barrel retreated, and Charles obediently jumped down then turned to help Eugenie slide out and stand up.

He had to steady her. The cold North wind whipped her hair around. Without permission he removed the gag. She cast him a grateful look and worked her jaw as if it were stiff.

"Here now," the young man holding the musket said. "You oughtn't to have done that."

She glared at him. "Jamey, are you not ashamed? I thought you liked working for me."

He looked ashamed. "I do, ma'am. I did. But my uncle said—."

"Enough," Poulaine said as he came up behind them. "Colonel, you should not have removed her gag."

"Out here," his glance encompassed the vast sea before them and the empty land around them and the greying clouds overhead, "no one will hear if she screams for help."

Poulaine looked around. "Come, we are to be met. The path is over here."

Charles steadied Eugenie on the path. Her hands clutched at his

Epilogue ~ Saturday, 22 March 1812

Toby walked straight into the vicarage, past her mother, past her brothers, past her sister who had the wits to say, "In the garden."

He veered and cut through the breakfast room.

And there she was, staring at the cherub statuette as if it needed a lesson in clothing.

At his heavy steps, she turned and broke into a smile. Melly's smile wavered when she saw the damage to his face. "You're hurt? Are Eugenie and Col. Audley safe?"

He swept past the question, swept her into his arms, and kissed her as if his life depended on her.

As it did, Toby realized when he lifted his head. Her bemused expression flooded him with satisfaction.

He pulled the ring on its ribbon from beneath his shirt, untied it, and took her left hand.

Melly caught her breath then looked up, returning his gaze as he slipped the ring on her finger.

"At last," she said.

"At last?"

"Isn't that what you were thinking, Toby?"

"Partly." He scooped her up and headed for the bench in the arbor. "I had a few thoughts in this direction." And his Melly giggled and looped her arms around his neck.

. ~ . ~ . ~ .

"What kind of wedding do you need?"

They had gone no farther than his study. Charles had refused to let Eugenie out of sight, so the Rev. Ratcliffe had taken them to Ridings before rolling Poulaine's confiscated carriage back to the village.

Eugenie had protested her sandy state, but Charles had towed her behind him. "I need to hold you," he muttered as he drew her onto the sofa.

She settled beside him, thinking to humor him for a few minutes, only to wake hours later, the sun blazing through the windows.

When she had shifted, appalled at the time and her still-sandy clothes and shoes, Charles had tightened his arms. "Not yet." He inhaled deeply then said, "What kind of wedding do you need?"

She nestled her head on his shoulder. "You have not proposed, and you ask about the wedding? Englishmen!"

"I'm not going to propose to you."

"*Tiens*? Perhaps a woman wishes for something more than a whispered declaration of love before a fight occurs."

"You will have my words of love every day for the rest of our lives."

"Oh. *Bon. Eh bien*, what kind of wedding do I want?"

"No. What kind of wedding do you need? I need to hold you every night and every morning and every noon. I need to hold you now and never let go. I need the wedding over yesterday, but I will settle for an Ordinary License and a wedding tomorrow morning."

Eugenie leaned back to search his face, with its lines crinkling around his tawny eyes and his mouth curved slightly. "*Mon Dieu, tu es vraiment serieuse!* It *is* a declaration."

"*Ce n'est pas un reve; c'est la réalité*," he retorted.

She thought back to their conversation at the Cables, the first time he had made an effort to speak with her. A month had not passed, and he was not proposing; he was *telling* her they were going to marry. "Charles, do you truly want an Ordinary License instead of the Banns?"

"No, I want the wedding today, so I can hold you tonight, but the closest to that is an Ordinary License and a Sunday morning wedding, so that is what I need. Eugenie, you blush adorably. Will you blush after our wedding night?"

"Charles! This is not—it is not—*ce n'est pas comme il faut*! *Tout le monde*, they will attend the church in the morning. When they see our vows, they will believe we rush to marriage."

"Exactly. Do you care what they believe? I want you. I love you. I need you."

She closed her jaw with a snap. A better proposal she could not imagine, and his pressing for haste showed his ardency. Had he not said, when they were facing death, that he would never again hesitate to reach for his desires? She should be so brave. After all, she loved him with the same needy desire.

"Charles," she swallowed. A clog in her throat threatened to dam the words, but she forced them out. "I need you. I need to hold you every night and every morning and every noon." His arms tightened around her, and tension seeped out of him. "I will accept an Ordinary License."

"Good then. Tomorrow morning my carriage will come for you by nine. The vicar will marry us."

"In front of the whole parish?"

"Yes." His voice held fat satisfaction. "My cook will have the wedding breakfast prepared. We'll invite the Ratcliffes and Mr. Kennit and the Cables and most definitely the Montagues. And anyone else who wants to toast our happiness." He shifted her, settling her even closer. "And by teatime I will have discovered how many times I can make you blush."

"Charles!"

He stopped her mouth with a kiss, and very quickly she didn't care who he intended to invite to the wedding breakfast.

. ~ . ~ . ~ .

Sir Roger Nazenby re-folded the letter from Tobias Kennit and let it drop into the flames.

A deep satisfaction filled him. Once again, his people had foiled a French operation. The odds continued to tip in their favor.

Poulaine hadn't entered blind, working all by himself through London, using contacts, finding sources, committing murders. No. Poulaine had had help, clever help, with threads spun into many parts of London and Britain.

A French spymaster. The man who had replaced Claude Thierry.

Perhaps Claude Thierry had actually worked for this man.

This French spymaster man remained, likely based here in London. A master spider who wove his sticky web all over, he remained elusive—for now. His agents would have to act; their actions would leave threads. Some would be sticky, collecting information to send back to France. Some would be darkly venomous, leaving more bodies, the way Poulaine had murdered one person after another in his search for Audley.

Sir Roger would remember every sticky thread, every poisonous action. He would track all of them to the web spun by the spidery spymaster.

And he would eliminate this threat to Britain.

. ~ . ~ . ~ .

Thank You*!*

Thank you for reading ***The Danger for Spies***.

The first book in the series *A Game of Secrets* was a providential story that helped me to survive one of the darkest times in my life. Still to this day, many years later, I am amazed at the hope every scene of that story offered to me during my writing. Then came *A Game of Spies*, as I reached the conclusion of that dark time, another inspired gift that turned my eyes away from the past and toward the future.

When contemplating self-publishing, way back in 2013, from the manuscripts that I had tinkered with over the years, I selected *A Game of Secrets* and *A Game of Spies* as my launch books. I knew, however, that I would need another book to assist the launch, and in the next year I penned *A Game of Hearts* ~~ and thus was born the idea of a loosely connected series of novels, the **Hearts in Hazard**.

When I published these first three books in 2015, I thought I was finished with the conflict of French spies. I was wrong, for *The Danger for Spies* very quickly picked up one of the stray threads from *Game of Spies*.

Again I thought I was through—but again, I was wrong. I had left more dangling threads, which became *The Hazard for Spies* after a couple of years of percolation.

Any reader will tell you that they have a favorite author and a favorite series by that author and favorite books within a series. I did expect that to happen with the **Hearts in Hazard** series, and some books are dearer to my heart than others (usually the ones with unexpected storylines). I never expected to fall in love with every one of the books and every one of the protagonists. See, wrong again!

With the **Hearts in Hazard** series coming to its projected end, I'm experiencing a strange sadness :: "Don't go yet," it says. Maybe that sadness is telling me that I'm not finished after all. *The Hazard for Spies* does introduce three characters that I want to explore in the future—yet even if I do, they will not be part of the **HnH** series but will have their own series—because the time frame will shift forward about ten to fifteen years.

The last projected book of **Hearts in Hazard**, book 12, is *The Hazard of Hearts,* a true vintage gothic ~ *Two wives haunt the castle. Will she be the third to die?* This will join the other **HnH** books that are more like the vintage gothics of Victoria Holt and Dorothy Eden. The first in that style is *The Dangers to Hearts* (picking up the character of Jess Carter from *The Game of Secrets)*, followed by *The Key to Secrets* (introducing Constable Hector Evans) and *The Key with Hearts*.

Read on for a snippet list of all the books in the **Hearts in Hazard** series as well as my **Into Death** series, set after World War I.

For any questions, comments, and speculations about any of my books, please contact winkbooks@aol.com.

You can find my books on my Amazon author page or my website ~~ www.writersinkbooks.com

To receive monthly information about all of my books, please join my monthly newsletter list. Contact me at winkbooks@aol.com and receive a free peak of the book I am currently writing. I won't pester you with affiliate links or pass your email to any other person or institution. Promise!

Indie writers thrive on reviews. With *any* book that you enjoy, please share with other readers looking for escape from the stresses of life.

Dream it. Believe it. Do it.

~~ *M.A. Lee*

French Spies Threaten British Lives

In the **Hearts in Hazard** series, the four interconnected books on locating French spies are these ~

1st Book ~ A Game of Secrets

Smugglers, secrets and spies: Kate tries to hide in plain sight; Tony tries to catch a spy. First they fall in love, then they fall into trouble with smugglers. Will they survive?

Kate Charteris never expects to become a damsel in distress, yet she must escape her cousin's unwanted attentions. While she might be orphaned in Regency England, she is no damsel who faints at the first sight of a dragon-like trouble.

On the hunt for the lair of smugglers and spies for Napoleon, Tony Farraday never expects to fall hard for a damsel not quite in distress. When he collides with Kate on a street corner, he is instantly attracted to her. Yet Kate must catch the mail coach before it leaves, and Tony still needs orders from the spycatcher Giles Hargreaves.

Neither expects to meet again at a run-down inn on the English coast. On a crumbling cliffside, they vow to pretend to be strangers. Yet their attraction turns into a flame, jeopardizing their secrets.

Then they discover they are in the lair of smugglers used by the French spy. Will the smugglers end their dangerous game of secrets? Or will both Kate and Tony be caught in a watery trap with a watery end when the smugglers sail for France? Have they both lost this *Game of Secrets*?

2nd Book ~~ A Game of Spies

Enter A Game of Spies, where the salons and soirées of Regency England are countered by spies and gambling.

Josette Sourantine expects only dancing, flirtations, and gambling on cards when she visits her widowed sister-in-law in London. Her talent with cards quickly attracts the attention of the rake Tobias Kennit and the handsome society prize Lord Gordon Musgrove.

Giles Hargreaves searches the London salons for a spy sending vital government documents to agents for Napoleon. He focuses on the salons hosted by the *émigré* Sourantine family, never expecting to enjoy his flirtation with a young woman who could be the spy he's looking for.

When their flirtation turns into a light dalliance, Giles wonders if he has fallen for a traitor to England. Josette fears she is giving her heart to a hardened rake. How can he declare his love when they have known each other so briefly?

How will they discover the truth? Or will the French spies give their own answer to that question?

3rd Book ~~ The Dangers for Spies ~~

This Book

4th Book ~~ The Hazards for Spies

Disguised to Spy. ~ A young constable tracks treacherous traitors. A spinster hopes to find a killer. Will murder destroy their chance for love?

Conrad Hoppock left his village and the girl he secretly loved for a chance at a better livelihood. He joined the London constabulary and began working with the Bow Street Runners. Now he hunts the master spy stealing information for Bonapartist France. His search sends him undercover in a lawyer's office.

When Phinney Darracott's sister and brother-in-law died, their children whispered "murder". She dismissed that claim as unreasonable terrors caused by the tragic loss. Yet after repeated burglaries and an arson that destroyed their home, Phinney believed the whispers. Now she wants justice for their murders.

The clues lead her to London. There, she disguises herself as a cleaning maid for the very law office where Conrad is disguised as a clerk. Phinney's young niece Elise and the street urchin Vic secretly pursue a different tangle of clues to the murders.

In the night hours, when all is still, Phinney prowls for the evidence. Then she encounters Conrad.

And the lawyer at the center of the tangle of clues is shot dead while they watch from their hiding place.

Can Conrad discover the identity of the French mastermind? Will Phinney's single-minded pursuit lead her into the murderer's snare? Will the children be caught and sold into London's underworld?

Will they discover the connection between past and present murders?

Or will two bullets allow the murderer and the French master spy to continue their work against the British government?

Hearts in Hazard by M.A. Lee

Mysteries with a dash of romance, set during the Regency Era of England

1 ~ *A Game of Secrets* ~ Smugglers, secrets and spies: Kate tries to hide in plain sight; Tony tries to catch a spy. First they fall in love, then they fall into trouble with smugglers. Will they survive?

2 ~ *A Game of Spies* ~ Salons and soirées, flirtation and dancing, gambling and spies: Josette and Giles fall in love over a deck of cards—and try not to die.

Spymaster Giles Hargreaves was introduced in *A Game of Secrets*.

3 ~ *A Game of Hearts* ~ **Two couples** :: One titled widow, one wealthy businessman: two hearts shadowed by their past. One bright young flirt, one hard-edged young man: two hearts crossed by circumstance. Mix in a courtesan and two rakes, all out for mischief, and murder bloody and foul.

4 ~ *The Danger of Secrets* ~ Deep in the wintry countryside, a house warmed by relatives and friends: secrets of family, secrets of hearts, secrets of blood and pain. Match a daughter to an unknown father; match a spinster to an earl; match a serial killer to his next victim.

Gordon Musgrove was introduced in *A Game of Spies*.

5 ~ *The Danger for Spies* ~ Impossibilities? Rakes don't lose their hearts. Spies don't give up the game. No one hides in plain sight. Codes are unbreakable. A man can't hold onto revenge for years and years. Impossibilities are designed to be shattered.

Toby Kennitt was introduced in *A Game of Spies*.

6 ~ *The Danger to Hearts* ~ A country manor in early Spring: older woman and younger man. Horses, cats, needlework, roses and afternoon teas ~ What could possibly go wrong in an idyll? Trouble in the past, trouble now, and murder.

The character Jess Carter was introduced in *A Game of Secrets*.

7 ~ *The Key to Secrets* ~ Debutantes should snare fiancés, not murder them. Constable Hector Evans must solve three murders. Is his former love guilty, of is she a convenient scapegoat?

Constable Hector Evans was introduced in *The Danger to Hearts*.

8 ~ *The Key for Spies* ~ Spies and traitors. Lies and treachery. Unexpected love where bullets fly. One traitor destroys loyalty. What will two traitors destroy?

9 ~ *The Key for Hearts* ~ A convenient marriage inconveniently causes murder.

10 ~ *The Hazard of Secrets*. Two hearts with dangerous pasts—Can they keep their secrets, or will murder force them to reveal all?

11 ~ *The Hazard for Spies* ~ Disguised to spy. Will murder destroy their chance for love?

12 ~ *The Hazard for Hearts* ~ Two wives haunt the castle. Will she be the third to die?

The **Into Death** Series, set after World War I

Digging into Death ~ A governess seeking refuge, a handsome young man, an archaeological dig: romance is inevitable; murder is not. Suspicions escalate, artifacts are stolen, and then a second murder. Has the love of her life beguiled her straight into death? Available in paperback and e-book

Christmas with Death ~ Christmas is for miracles, merriment, and murder. Set in 1919 at an English country manor for a party throughout Christmastide. Available in paperback and e-book.

Portrait with Death, publishing soon ~ the conclusion of the Isabella Newcombe series

Nonfiction by M.A. Lee

Think like a Pro Writer series

Old Geeky Greeks: Write Stories with Ancient Techniques ~ Storytelling has its roots in the strong foundations of classical antiquity. Avoid the re-packaged "exclusive insights" and "wham-pow webinars" and return to the source, organized as a seminar in book form.

Think like a Pro: New Advent for Writers ~ Seven lessons to guide your growth from newbie writer to "thinking like a pro writer". Now available in paperback and e-book.

Think / Pro: A Planner for Writers ~ An undated planner with daily word counts, progress meters, project planning, and goals analysis. Paperback only. How else will you record your goals and progress?

Discovering Your Novel ~ a 52-week course for new writers, offering guidance from original idea to publication and marketing.

Discovering Characters ~ Delving deeply into your primary characters entails more than just templates and character interviews. You also need to know your secondary characters. Focus on more than appearance, more than intellect, and explore your characters hearts and souls. Discover them!

Discovering Your Plot ~ What writers need and want for plot structures and genre expectations. Control pacing, tension, and suspense with a stronger comprehension of the major sections of a novel.

Discovering your Author Brand ~ The greatest secret to catch the attention of fly-by readers? Branding. Writers need to brand their books, their series, and themselves as the author. Packed with examples and explanations from past successful marketing efforts.

Discovering Sentence Craft ~ Zeug-what? Chiasmus? Auxesis? Are those spelled correctly? Well, yes. These are literary devices used for centuries by the best writers to make their works memorable. Writers are artists, seeking ideas from the creative muse. We're also crafters, looking for the best ways to present those creative ideas. *DiscS~Craft* presents techniques for using figurative & interpretive concepts as well as the structures of inversions, repetitions, oppositions, and sequencings.

Just Start Writing :: Inspiration 4 Writers, book 1 ~Writing can be a dizzy whirl of a carousel, all colors and mirrors with unicorns and griffins and dragons to ride. How do you get your ticket, climb on the carousel, and join the writing ride? If you want to pursue your writing dream, *Just Start Writing* will help you start.

2 * 0 * 4 Lifestyle series

2 * 0 * 4 Lifestyle: A Planner for Living ~ *Intermittent fasting. Bible Journaling. Keto Diet. 7-Minute Workout. Five minutes with God.* If the newest fads to follow are leaving you cold and edgy, time to re-think your daily plan. Return to Luke 10:27 to involve the whole self—heart, soul, mind & body. 2 * 0 * 4 offers an undated planner to help you muse and move, feast and fast, and live and love. Paperback only. How else will you write in it? Available in the Meadow and the Mountain River editions.

Pen Names of M.A. Lee

Remi Black ~ Fae Mark'd
The Fae Mark'd Wizard
Weave a Wizardry Web
Dream a Deadly Dream
Sing a Graveyard Song
Kindle a Fae's Wrath (coming soon)
Quench a Dragon's Fire (in the sketching stage)
Dance to Bone-Edged Music (in the sketching stage)

Fae Mark'd World
To Wield the Wind :: Spells of Air 1
To Charm the Air: Spells of Air 2 (coming soon)
To Curse the Wyre: Spells of Air 3 (sketching stage)

Edie Roones ~ Seasons in Sansward
Summer Sieges
Autumn Spells
Winter Sorcery
Spring Magicks (in the sketching stage)

All books from Writers' Ink are available at Amazon and other online distributors.

For any comments, questions, and speculations, contact winkbooks@aol.com. Use the subject line to direct your email to a specific book or series.

www.ingramcontent.com/pod-product-compliance
Lightning Source LLC
Chambersburg PA
CBHW020914180626
46816CB00007BA/2403